"YOU'RE BLEEDING AGAIN," JOHANNA SAID with a soft gasp, and stepped toward him.

"Leave it," Dylan growled, grabbing her hand when she reached for him. He didn't want her pity, or her ministering to him like he was some invalid. What he wanted, wanted so very badly, was her kiss.

"But you're injured," she said, standing very still in front of him.

"It's not going to kill me." The bones in her wrist were small and delicate; he could feel her pulse beating in the palm of his hand, racing. With his free hand he traced the cool, sweet curve of her jaw.

"But it's making you hurt," Johanna said, trembling from his touch, compassion, and anger that he didn't take better care of his life. She tried to pull her captured wrist free, but he held tight.

"The only hurt I'm worried about," Dylan said, his voice growing husky, his fingers curving around to cup her chin, "is if it's going to hurt me more to kiss you—or to let you go. . . ."

WHAT ARE *LOVESWEPT* ROMANCES?

They are stories of true romance and touching emotion. We believe those two very important ingredients are constants in our highly sensual and very believable stories in the LOVESWEPT *line. Our goal is to give you, the reader, stories of consistently high quality that may sometimes make you laugh, sometimes make you cry, but are always fresh and creative and contain many delightful surprises within their pages.*

Most romance fans read an enormous number of books. Those they truly love, they keep. Others may be traded with friends and soon forgotten. We hope that each LOVESWEPT *romance will be a treasure—a "keeper." We will always try to publish*

LOVE STORIES YOU'LL NEVER FORGET
BY AUTHORS YOU'LL ALWAYS REMEMBER

The Editors

Loveswept® 653

AVENGING ANGEL

GLENNA McREYNOLDS

BANTAM BOOKS

NEW YORK · TORONTO · LONDON · SYDNEY · AUCKLAND

AVENGING ANGEL

A Bantam Book / November 1993

*Loveswept
Bantam Books
P.O. Box 985
Hicksville, NY 11802*

ISBN 0-553-44353-4

Published simultaneously in the United States and Canada

*Bantam Books are published by Bantam Books, a division of Bantam Dou-
bleday Dell Publishing Group, Inc. Its trademark, consisting of the words
"Bantam Books" and the portrayal of a rooster, is Registered in U.S. Patent
and Trademark Office and in other countries. Marca Registrada. Bantam
Books, 1540 Broadway, New York, New York 10036.*

PRINTED IN THE UNITED STATES OF AMERICA

OPM   0 9 8 7 6 5 4 3 2 1

To Roger—my main squeeze
at Trivia Central.
Thank you and thank you again.

ONE

The woman. He needed her . . . desperately. He needed her to drag him up, get him out, and set him free.

Dylan drove with nerveless precision, tearing down the highway, burning up the road and the tires on his black Mustang. Wind whipped his hair through the open window and stung his face with the blast-furnace force of a summer gone crazy with heat. From Chicago, to Lincoln, Nebraska, to Colorado, the asphalt had shimmered to the horizon like the shadow of a mirage on the landscape.

Without taking his eyes from the road, he lifted a Styrofoam cup to his mouth and drained it of coffee. He'd lost the other two times he'd broken his FBI cover to prevent disaster. He'd been too late, too slow, in far too deep to surface in time to save a life. He wouldn't be too late to save Johanna Lane.

He couldn't be. He'd come up for good and three was his lucky number.

A grim line broke across his face, an expression no one had ever mistaken for a smile. Since when did he know about luck? He had no luck.

In the darkness ahead, a pickup truck pulled onto the highway. Dylan hissed an obscenity, his fist crushing the empty cup before he threw it to the floor. The man had to be blind not to see the Mustang hurtling toward him. When the driver didn't even speed up to the limit, Dylan cursed him again, taking a lot of names in vain and ending up with half a dozen synonyms of dirty slang for sex.

The oncoming traffic was heavy on the two-lane highway outside Boulder, but Dylan had no time and nothing left to lose except his pulse. Flooring the gas pedal, he roared up on the truck and at the last moment jerked the wheel, sending the Mustang slewing into the other other lane, taking a highly calculated risk and the narrowest of openings in the traffic. Cars scattered onto the shoulder. The truck skidded off the road.

Hard-won skill, not luck, guided Dylan through the hundred-mile-an-hour maze he'd made of a van, a station wagon, and two compacts. Dylan Jones had no luck.

The fact was proved a mile down the road, less than a minute's worth of traveling time. The flashing lights of a police car lit up his back window and rearview mirror like a Fourth of July parade.

Dylan swore again and pressed harder on the gas

pedal, willing the Mustang to greater speed. The city lights of Boulder were seconds away. He'd come too far, too fast, too hard to lose.

He swept through the first stoplight on the north side of town, ignoring its red color. The Mustang barely held on to the ninety-degree turn he slammed it through. The tires squealed and smoked on the hot pavement. The chassis shuddered. Working the steering wheel one way and then the other, he missed hitting a car in the eastbound lane and shot between two westbound vehicles.

The police car behind him missed the turn and came to a jolting stop in the middle of the intersection, siren and lights going full bore, snarling traffic even further. Dylan made the second left-hand turn he saw, then wound through the streets in a frenzied, seemingly haphazard fashion for more than a mile. Finally he slowed the Mustang to a stop on a side street, pulling between two other vehicles, a gray, nondescript sedan and a midsize truck.

The summer night was quiet except for the pounding of his own heart. Expensive houses crowded this part of town. Porch lights were on, smaller, homier versions of the street lamps, but the interiors of the houses were dark. People were settled in for the night, safe, sound, and unsuspecting.

He waited for a moment, checking the street before pulling his duffel bag across the front seat to his lap and slipping his left arm out of his coat. The bag was heavier than clothes would have allowed, the weight being made up in firepower and ordnance. It was the only protection he had, and it felt like damn little compared with what he was up against.

Sweat trickled down the side of his face. At the corner of his eye, the moisture found the day-old cut angling from his temple to his ear. The salty drops slid into the groove, burning the raw skin. He swiped at the irritation with the back of his hand, then yanked open the duffel.

He took out a shortened, pump-action twelve-gauge shotgun and slipped the gun's strap over his free shoulder. After angling the shotgun down the side of his torso, he put his arm back through his coat sleeve. The duffel went over his other shoulder as he got out of the car. The policeman had been behind him long enough to call in his plates. The Mustang had to be ditched. It didn't matter. If he lost Johanna Lane, he didn't much care if he got through the night with his life. He sure as hell didn't care if he got out with his car.

He walked to the pickup truck in front of him and tried the door, his gaze moving constantly, checking shadows and sounds. The door was locked. The owner of the late-model gray sedan parked behind him wasn't nearly as cautious. He got in and smashed the ignition assembly with the butt of the shotgun. Then he went to work hot-wiring the car.

Johanna Lane lived at 300 Briarwood Court, and Dylan knew exactly where 300 Briarwood Court was in relation to his current position—two blocks west and one half block north.

❖━━━━━❖

Johanna Lane stood on her third-floor balcony overlooking the street. French doors were open behind her, allowing the night wind to lift and flutter sheer, floor-length curtains. Vivaldi's *Four Seasons* played on the stereo, the classical notes crystal clear, floating on the air with all the purity that the finest digital sound was capable of producing. The stereo system was an indulgence, one of many in the oak-floored, art-deco-furnished apartment.

She turned partway to look inside. In the dining room, an unfinished, candlelit dinner of pasta alfredo and salad was neatly laid out on one end of an intricately carved, black lacquer table. A damask napkin was crumpled next to the still-full crystal wineglass.

She really should eat, she thought, watching the candle flame dip and bow with the breeze. If she wasn't going to run home to Chicago and her father, she should eat, and she'd decided against running. Running was an admission of guilt, either of a crime she'd been very careful not to commit, or of an act of betrayal she'd never considered.

Austin Bridgeman was flying in from Chicago. To do some follow-up work on a deal that had gone bad in Boulder, he'd said when he called. He'd suggested going out for drinks or a late dinner so they could talk about old times—old times when she had worked for him as his most private legal counsel.

Even the thought of her previous employment made her head ache and her palms sweat. She'd left her job and Chicago because of what Austin Bridgeman had become, and she doubted if the intervening four months had improved his moral character.

Slowly, to calm herself, she closed her eyes and took a deep breath. In four years of working for Austin, she'd seen him skirt the law many, many times, bending it at will with his power and his money. She'd seen him crawl on his belly like a snake to make bribery look like a gift. She'd seen him voice requests as unrepentant demands to politicians and judges alike. But she hadn't seen him break a law until two days earlier, Friday morning, when she'd read the front-page newspaper story about a senator charged with influence peddling. With all the other congressional scandals cropping up, she hadn't given the story much more than a glance at first. Then a name had caught her eye, the name of a small, privately held company in Illinois—Morrow Warner.

The influence the dear senator had been peddling went far beyond the expected pork barreling. He had dabbled in foreign affairs and foreign wars, foreign corporations, foreign currency, and especially foreign imports. The press had labeled him the "Global Connection," and all of his hard work had been directed toward filling the coffers of Morrow Warner.

Johanna knew who owned Morrow Warner. She also knew that no one else did, because she had hidden the owner's identity in miles of paperwork, barely skirting the law herself. A precaution, Austin had said, something for his old age, something the board of directors of Bridgeman, Inc., couldn't take away.

Saturday's paper had confirmed worse than influence peddling by the senator and had alleged extortion. Then that morning's Sunday *Post* had quoted "reliable sources" confirming extortion and alleging underworld connections and a possible tie-in to an assassination. Two hours after she'd read the article, Austin had called wanting to visit her, personally, that night.

Johanna had thought about notifying the police, then realized irrationality wasn't her best option. Austin hadn't been charged with anything, and asking someone to dinner didn't qualify as a crime. Powerful men were easy targets for scandal and allegations. Both the Illinois senator and Austin Bridgeman were powerful men. She knew better than to jump to conclusions, or to believe everything she read in the newspapers.

Still, she wished her law partner, Henry Wayland, had decided to stay in Boulder for the weekend just this once. She would like someone to be with her when Austin came, since she'd decided to beg off dinner, and drinks, and especially long talks about old times. The best posture for her to assume was one of cool formality and discretion.

At least that's what she'd thought earlier. Now darkness had fallen and she wasn't sure.

In a distracted gesture, she ran her hand back through her hair. Damn Henry for disappearing every Friday. She knew he did it to escape his mother, but that was ridiculous for a grown man. She didn't even know where he was. All she knew was that he'd be back by Monday morning at 9:00 A.M. sharp. Henry was nothing if not reliable.

Austin was reliable, too, but not in a comfortable way. She had worked for a powerful man. She knew power corrupted; she'd seen the workings of corruption firsthand.

Assassination. It was improbable . . . but was it possible?

She had seen Austin break men with less thought than some people gave to lunch. A few times she'd helped him. It was part of the game of high-stakes business. Winner take all. Losers run like hell.

She wasn't running. She could handle Austin.

She turned back toward the street. The only movement was a gray sedan cruising the block at a crawl, no doubt looking for the rare parking spot.

Raising her chin, she rolled her head to one side, easing the ache of muscles gone tight with strain. She continued the motion by lifting her hair off the back of her neck to let the night wind blow against her skin. It was so damn hot.

Her suitcases were still packed in her bedroom. She probably should have run.

She probably should have run like hell.

Dylan watched her with a narrowed gaze, taking in every sinuous line, every sultry curve. She made jeans look like custom-tailored slacks and a silk T-shirt look like a thousand dollars' worth of handwork. It was Johanna Lane all right. Pure sweet class from the sheen of her honey-blond hair to the arch of her foot, which he'd previously seen only encased in butter-soft, Italian leather heels. He remembered everything about her, everything he'd seen at a distance. Austin's rough boys weren't allowed to fraternize with the upper echelons of the hierarchy. He doubted if Johanna Lane remembered he existed. He hoped not. It would only make things harder—on him.

He opened the duffel bag and took out a wide roll of cloth tape. Tearing off a length, he taped the passenger-door handle to a random spot beneath the dash. The rest of the roll went in his overcoat. He didn't have time to talk her into going anywhere. Nor was he particularly inclined toward explanations. He hurt too damn bad. He'd been two days without sleep, almost as long without food, and he was bleeding again. He could feel the fresh dampness seeping down the right side of his chest. He'd killed a man last night in Lincoln, but not before the bastard had cut him.

Get out. Get out while you can, his conscience whispered. Then he remembered he didn't have a conscience. He'd killed a man in Lincoln to save a worthless life—his own—and maybe one that was worth a whole lot more, Johanna Lane's.

He turned and, with a quick jab of the gun, broke the dome light in the sedan. The last thing he needed was a welcome-home signal when he brought her out.

❧———❧

Johanna closed and locked the French doors, then pulled the sheers and the drapes. She'd packed her suitcases on a gut instinct, and the later it got, the more rational her instinct seemed. If she hurried, she could still catch a flight to Chicago. Once she was safe in her parents' big house, Austin Bridgeman would look more manageable. And it had occurred to her more than once that she might end up needing a good lawyer. Her father happened to be the best.

In the bathroom, she threw her toothbrush, comb, and makeup into a small bag. Before she put in the aspirin bottle, she shook two pills into her hand, then a third. It was definitely turning out to be a three-aspirin night.

She swallowed the pills with a glass of water and left the water running for a second glass. The heat had been oppressive all day, and not even night had lowered the record temperatures.

A sound in the living room drew her head around. She shut the water off and listened again, concentrating, trying to hear over the sudden pounding of her heart and the rush of adrenaline pumping through her body.

When no more sound was forthcoming, she forced herself to relax enough to think. Her first thought was to find something to defend herself with, and she grabbed her longest nail file, the most lethal thing she could find in the whole damn bathroom. She told herself she was overreacting, but her fingers wrapped and tightened around the file as if it were a knife.

She stepped quietly into the hall, listening. If anything looked even remotely amiss in the apartment, she would slip out the front door and leave. She wasn't going to take chances. If Austin had sent someone in his place, someone who didn't ring doorbells and use front doors, she needed protection.

She reached the arch connecting the hall and the living room and peeked around the corner.

"Ahhh!" The file clattered to the floor, dropped by fingers numbed from a quick, well-placed blow. Her next cry was smothered by a large, strong hand. An even stronger arm went around her middle, crushing her to her assailant's body.

"My name is Dylan, Dylan Jones," a harsh voice whispered in her ear. "I've been a lot of things in my life, but a rapist isn't one of them. So ease your mind. I don't want to hurt you."

She squirmed violently in his arms, but his strength was indomitable.

"Your name is Johanna Lane," the voice continued, "and four months ago you worked for Austin Bridgeman. You need to decide if you're going to cooperate, or if we're leaving here the hard way."

Johanna stilled. Austin *had* sent someone else. She squeezed her eyes shut for an instant, fear and anger at her own stupidity washing through her. She should have run.

"Feel that?" her captor asked, his voice breathless and gravelly.

Something pushed against her hip, and she nodded.

"It's a twelve-gauge shotgun, and I am definitely

threatening you. We're going out into the hall, into the elevator, and out the front door. That's cooperation. The hard way is with you unconscious, or taped up, or both." He lifted the gun and rested the barrel against her temple. "Do you want to do this the hard way?"

She shook her head once, very slowly. He'd said he didn't want to hurt her; he'd also made it clear he would hurt her if he felt the need. She was too frightened to believe the first statement, and too frightened not to believe the second.

"Good." He stepped back toward the door, holding her tight against him while he opened it a crack and checked the hall. "Go."

They moved toward the bank of elevators, his body propelling her forward, pushing her from behind, overriding her faltering gait. The gun wasn't at her temple. She didn't know where it was, but she didn't doubt its presence or his willingness to use it, yet she still wanted to scream and fight him. A greater fear kept her from doing either.

Dylan stayed behind her on the long walk down the hall, her body clasped to his. He kept behind her in the elevator, applying just enough pressure on her arm to let her know he wouldn't tolerate a struggle, not even the hint of one. He wasn't into terrorizing women, but he was committed to worse if she gave him any trouble. He knew Austin Bridgeman, and he knew he didn't have time to be nice.

The elevator doors whooshed open in the lobby. For a moment freedom was fifteen steps away. In the next instant it was gone. A group of men stepped into the pool of light illuminating the portico of the apartment building—with Austin Bridgeman leading the pack.

Dylan lunged for the "Close Door" button on the operating panel, shoving the woman away from him and into a corner of the elevator. He single-handedly pumped a shell into the chamber of the twelve-gauge, keeping the gun leveled at her and giving her a grim look.

Johanna pushed herself deeper into the corner of the elevator, instinctively widening the distance between herself and the man called Dylan Jones. The urge to scream receded to a dull, throbbing ache in the back of her throat. His eyes were brown, dark and bright with an overload of adrenaline. Beard stubble darkened his jaw. His light-colored hair was longer in back than in front, and in front it was standing on end, raked through and furrowed—wild, like the gleam in his eyes.

The mercury had pushed ninety-two that day, but he was wearing an overcoat, a lined overcoat stained with dirt . . . or blood. A torn black T-shirt molded his torso, soft black jeans clung to his hips and legs.

He was bruised on one side of his face and cut on the other. He was muscular and lean, hard, stripped down to the basics of strength. He was feral.

Dylan waited, listening and watching her size him up and grow more afraid. There was nothing but silence outside. Nothing but the noise of their ragged breathing inside. Then the mechanical sound of the other elevator moving intruded. Dylan steadied himself with a breath and removed his finger from the "Close Door" button. The doors slid open. He stepped out, ready.

Johanna heard a movement, a scuffle, and a muffled thud. Now was the time to scream, she told herself. Dylan Jones hadn't been sent by Austin. Austin had come in person to talk with her.

The thoughts had no sooner formed than she was jerked out of the elevator. The violence of the movement knocked the breath from her lungs. The speed with which he dragged her across the lobby, his hand tightly wound in a fistful of her shirt, the gun jammed against her ribs, kept her breathless. She stumbled, and he hauled her to her feet, always shoving her forward, keeping her fighting for her balance.

Out of the corner of her eye she saw the crumpled figure of a man lying next to the elevators. She tried once more to scream, but as if he'd known what her reaction would be, he moved his hand from her shirt to her neck and applied a warning pressure. She sobbed instead, and his hand immediately loosened, but only the barest of degrees.

He pushed the building doors open with his shoulder. Heat, sultry and intense, engulfed them. She stumbled again on the steps, and once again he kept her upright, on the thinnest edge of her balance.

Johanna knew now was the time to fight and kick, to scream and cry, but Dylan Jones never gave her the chance. He was a master at keeping her half off her feet and moving too fast to think. She did manage a hoarse moan, but a renewed pressure in her ribs with the gun barrel stifled the rest of her verbal rebellion.

They crossed the street, keeping to the shadows of the trees and the parked cars lining both sides of Briarwood Court. Johanna had chosen the neighborhood for the quiet elegance of the older homes and the architectural charm of the apartment building. For three blocks in either direction, Briarwood Court was a haven of upper-middle-class wealth. She had always felt secure and protected—until that night.

With a harshly voiced set of commands, Dylan directed her toward the gray sedan. "Get in on the driver's side. Don't mess around with me—just get in and scoot to the middle of the seat. Do *not* touch the passenger-side door. I've got it rigged to explode if it opens."

Her heart sank lower in her chest. There was no escaping him.

Dylan had a mental clock going in his head, and he knew Austin and his men were probably already heading back down to the street. He had not turned around to check if anyone had seen them from her balcony, but there was a chance someone had. He had checked the line of sight himself and knew the sedan, parked far up the street, was well hidden from view—if they could only get to it.

A commotion behind them, sounding like it came from the apartment building, had him speeding up their steps. He glanced once over his shoulder and started running, dragging her along with him. At the sedan, he shoved her into the front seat and slid in after her.

"Get down," he ordered, pinning her with the gun, then crawling over her as she was forced to the seat.

Johanna stiffened as they came into contact, body to body, with her on the bottom. In the dark, close interior of the car, he was overwhelmingly male and dangerous. He wasn't a big man, but his broad shoulders blocked all but the faintest light. His weight pressed her deep into the upholstery, paralyzing her as effectively as the gun barrel under her chin.

He looked over the back of the seat, through the rear window. He swore softly, then inched up her body, craning his neck to look out the passenger window. Johanna didn't move so much as a muscle fiber— until he came too close to the potentially lethal door.

Without conscious thought, her hand shot up and pressed against his chest, causing him to wince and swear again, not so softly.

"No," she whispered, putting force into the word instead of volume, her voice trembling.

When he looked down at her, she tilted her head toward the door and the trip wire of tape. He followed the gesture, and a heartbeat later the barest flicker of a smile touched his mouth, the most ironic smile she had ever seen. In that instant he looked familiar— incredibly familiar.

TWO

Dylan Jones . . . Dylan Jones. His name ran through her mind. She knew him. She was sure of it. The flash of memory set off by his smile was unmistakable, her intuition one hundred percent reliable. She was known for never forgetting a face. Still, she couldn't place him, couldn't put the name or the man into the right place, the right time.

She searched the face above her in the dim light, noting the gentle arch of his eyebrows, the straight line of his nose, the wry sensuality of his mouth—and another, more startling memory clicked into place. She'd not only known him, she'd been attracted to him.

The thought seemed unimaginable now, with his gun pressing on her body and him straddling her across the seat, trapping her. But she wasn't a woman given to casual attractions or casual flirtations, and her emotional memory bank was telling her she'd experienced both with him.

Where? Her gaze trailed back over his face. His smile had faded, and he was watching her with an intensity that unnerved her on very basic female levels. Her pulse picked up in speed and her awareness of him heightened. She'd seen that look before, delivered from across a room. She'd had the same reaction then, but in a place where she'd felt much safer than was possible now, with her actually lying beneath him. His look implied, though, both then and now, that she was exactly where he wanted her, where he needed her, where he'd dreamed of having her.

A frisson of fear coursed down her body as she acknowledged the unhidden message reflected in his eyes. She panicked and started to struggle.

"*No.* Don't." She gasped for a breath, pushing against him. "Stop."

With a lightninglike movement, he captured her hands in one of his and held her still. Dark lashes shadowed his eyes. His mouth tightened into a grim line, and his voice grew angry and soft. "I'm not trying to get in your pants, Miss Lane. I'm *trying* to save your life."

"No," she whispered.

Dylan swore and released her. He was the best damn liar he knew. His whole life was a lie. But he hadn't fooled her.

He swore again and looked out the window, but he didn't really see what he'd been trained to see.

The woman beneath him scrambled his brain. She always had.

Six months earlier he'd culminated four years of undercover work by slipping into Austin Bridgeman's underground empire as a bodyguard, a "security agent" for men who needed protecting. He had been highly recommended by his former employer, a man currently doing twenty years in a federal penitentiary compliments of Dylan. Dylan had been working toward taking Austin Bridgeman down the same way, with insider information and damning evidence compiled firsthand.

It had taken him a while to work himself up into the front office. When he'd gotten there, the first thing he'd noticed was Johanna Lane, a bombshell package of brains, legs, virtue, and sophistication. He'd spent the next eight weeks noticing everything about her and driving himself crazy by wanting something he couldn't have. He'd been almost relieved when she'd left the organization . . . almost.

He glanced back down at her. She was watching him with a wariness he respected. She was smart. He'd known that from the beginning. She was also clean, squeaky clean, the kind of clean a man like him craved after years of two-timing and double-dealing. In the course of his investigation, he'd found out a lot about her: She'd worked her way up from the bottom of Bridgeman, Inc.; she wasn't intimidated by Austin; she was damn good at her job. She also liked expensive perfume, the kind that warmed on a woman's skin and left her scent, subtle and evocative, lingering in the place where she'd been. She usually crossed her legs left over right, with a fluid, easy grace that had never failed to demand his attention.

His gaze slipped to her mouth. He knew how she put her lipstick on, the soft "O" her lips made, and the wild ideas it had given him. He knew she looked drop-dead serious and beautiful when she wore black.

He knew Austin had wanted her. Now Austin wanted her dead.

Dylan had been good at his job, too, and his job had been to fade into backgrounds and to be at Austin's beck and call. His job had been not to be noticed, but more than once he'd made sure Johanna noticed him. He'd made a point of being at meetings she had with Austin, especially toward the end of her tenure, when Austin had started coming on to her. He had always kept to his place, the farthest reaches of Austin's palatial office, ready to serve his employer—or to hang himself and his operation by coming to her rescue if Austin ever stepped over the line.

Dylan had never had to go that far. Johanna had handled Austin with the same blend of cool charm and studiousness she used with all of her business associates. Yet she had a vulnerability that had compelled Dylan to let her know he was on her side. He'd meet her eyes when Austin turned his back. He'd change his position, however slightly, whenever Austin got too friendly, subtly rearranging the dynamics of the room, deliberately shifting the focus of the tension. Then one night he'd found her alone in Austin's office, working late, finishing up business Austin needed for the next day. In twelve years of working for the FBI, he'd never made a mistake. He'd made two mistakes that night with Johanna Lane, and he'd known he was in deep, deep trouble.

Dylan checked the street again. Austin's men were fanning out along both sides. One man had been left guarding the entrance to the apartment building.

He took a deep breath, unintentionally increasing the contact between himself and the woman lying still beneath him. The fact did not go unnoticed, and he forced himself to concentrate on the men looking for them. He knew Austin's operating procedures inside out and backward. Jay, the man Dylan had downed by the elevators, would stay at the apartment building all night, until someone relieved him. Austin and the others would soon leave to organize the search from more comfortable quarters.

Dylan didn't have any illusions about how successful Austin would be in finding them. He'd tracked for Austin before, and the only advantage he had now was time. They would be found. All Dylan could do was choose the place, and hopefully stash the woman someplace safe before Austin caught up with them. When he went down, he wanted to go down alone.

He trained his eyes on the black limousine double-parked in front of the apartment building. Rodrigo, the newest "security agent" in Austin's empire, opened the rear door for his employer, then got in the driver's door and started the car.

Dylan slid back down behind the seat and over Johanna's body, covering her mouth with his hand.

"They're leaving. When they're gone, we'll leave. Remember"—he again smiled briefly—"don't open your door."

Johanna had no intention of opening her door. The man was dangerous, criminal in his kidnapping of her. She wouldn't put anything past him—except rape. She'd denied his statement to that effect, about getting in her pants and saving her life, but as she'd watched him her sense of familiarity had grown. When he'd smiled again, it had increased. If she could get him in some good light, clean him up, maybe she would recognize him.

What she would do after that remained a mystery. Austin had shown up at her apartment with four or five other men. She hadn't gotten a good count, but the group had seemed large, certainly larger than necessary or appropriate for a friendly get-together. Then Dylan Jones had said he was trying to save her life. And the first thing he'd done, she reminded herself, was give her his name. The facts might add up to Dylan Jones's side, if she knew who he was. On the other hand, over the last year of her employment with Bridgeman, Inc., Austin had taken to always having a few men around him for protection. Protection from what, she had never inquired, but the group of men he'd brought might only be his regular retinue.

"Okay," the man above her whispered, seemingly to himself, his gaze tracking what she couldn't see from her position. "We're moving out."

He pushed himself up and pulled her to a sitting position. The distance between them was still small, but every extra inch helped her gain a measure of composure. Whoever Dylan Jones was, he was somehow involved in Austin's problems. He wasn't a psychopathic maniac. He had a reason for kidnapping her, though whether it was to save her life, as he'd said, or to use her as a bargaining chip with Austin, she didn't know. But it was no coincidence that he'd shown up mere minutes ahead of her ex-employer.

"Where are you taking me?" she demanded in a shaky voice.

"Laramie," he said, surprising her with his candor.

"Wyoming?"

"The last time I checked." He reached under the steering wheel for the bare wires sticking out of a broken part on the steering column.

Johanna watched with growing unease as he sparked and twisted the wires together, starting the engine. The meaning of the unorthodox procedure wasn't lost on her.

"This isn't your car," she said.

He made no comment.

"Auto theft is a felony," she warned him, and he laughed, a short, dry sound.

The meaning of his laughter wasn't lost on her either. Grand theft auto was the least of his problems. Committing felonies came naturally.

How could she have met such a man? She wasn't a trial lawyer. She'd never been in court with a criminal. The closest she'd ever come to associating with shady people had been when Austin had started traveling with his crowd of bodyguards.

Her kidnapper steered the car onto the street, and she gave him a hesitant glance. His profile was shadowed, the bruise high on his cheekbone darker than the surrounding skin. They passed a street lamp, and its light cast a rim of luminosity on his forehead, nose, mouth, and chin. The light wove through the upended strands of his dark blond hair and caught the sheen of his eyes and the weariness therein.

Watching him, she unconsciously shook her head. Her memory was wrong. Her intuition had gone haywire. She didn't know Dylan Jones in any way. She took a deep, steadying breath and let it out. It was time to get some answers.

"Who are you?" she asked, turning her head so she was looking straight at him.

"Dylan Jones." He flipped on the turn signal and eased the sedan around a corner.

It was the answer she'd expected. Though she'd decided her earlier impression of familiarity had been wrong, a niggling doubt made her want to confirm her mistake.

"I get the feeling I know you. Why?" She used her most confrontational tone of voice, letting him know there was nothing pleasant about the feeling.

A muscle in his jaw tightened, and it took him a moment to answer, a moment in which she sensed he might not answer her at all.

"We've met," he finally said.

The admission hit her hard, like a falling wall of bricks, though she didn't believe him for a minute. She couldn't possibly have ever met him.

"Where?" she asked when she found her voice.

This time his answer was a lot longer in coming and consisted entirely of that oh-so-familiar smile, at once wry and loaded with mystery, leveled at her from across the short stretch of seat separating them.

He was lying, she decided. He had to be lying.

"If you release me now, things will go a lot easier for you," she said, forcing herself to use her calmest, most professional tone. It took effort to achieve, great effort, and got her exactly nothing.

His smile curled, and he flicked her a desultory glance, silently confirming what she'd suspected. He wasn't a fool. She was going throw the book at him the instant the first opportunity arose, and he knew it.

Dylan knew it, all right. He'd seen her in action. She would have him skinned and hung out to dry if he couldn't convince her he had damn good reasons for what he'd done, and if Austin didn't get to him first.

His money was on Austin.

He shifted his body behind the steering wheel, trying to find a comfortable position. It was impossible. Every square inch of him ached.

"Stop the car," she said suddenly, as if she hoped surprising him would garner her some cooperation.

It didn't.

"I can't do that," he said, unfazed by her demand.

"Why not, dammit?" She sounded near hysterics. "Why not just stop this damn car and let me go?"

Dylan allowed himself a shallow sigh. "Because there's a man back there with a gun."

"There's a man in here with a gun," she retorted, her voice sharp with frustration and frayed nerves.

"Yeah. But this man isn't quite as likely to use it on you as that man."

As reassurance, he knew it was damn little, but it was all he felt like offering. He didn't want her to like him. He didn't want her gratitude. He didn't want her to remember.

He'd broken his cover to save the lawyer Austin had decided was at the root of his crumbling empire. Now he was a dead man on borrowed time. But she didn't need to know anything about him, except at the end, when she might know he'd saved her life.

"Please . . ." The whispered word came at him in the darkness, surprising him with its intense yearning, and undermining his resolve as no amount of demands could. Her voice was so soft, so husky and sweet, the way he remembered from a long-ago night when she'd whispered that word to him with her mouth almost touching his.

He remembered the silky feel of her skin beneath his hands, the erotic way her breath had caught when he'd moved closer, tempted beyond reason to take what he wanted. Her scent had wound its way around him, increasing his pleasure, heightening his anticipation. They'd been so close, her breasts touching his chest, his hand cupping her face, ready to draw her into his kiss.

Dylan swore under his breath. That had been his first mistake: wanting her beyond reason. His second mistake had been not taking her.

THREE

Johanna was a city girl, born and bred in Chicago. She did not particularly care for wilderness, and Laramie, Wyoming, classified as such in her book. For miles she'd seen nothing but dark sky, stars, and rolling prairie, with hardly a light since they'd crossed the Colorado–Wyoming border. There were lights in Laramie, but not enough to calm a city girl's heart.

Neither was the company. Dylan Jones had gone mute before they'd gotten out of Boulder, and she'd be damned if she broke the silence first, not after her unforgivable moment of weakness. She felt like a fool for pleading with him. It wasn't like her to plead.

Her gaze slid to him. For a man supposedly trying to save her life, presumably from Austin, he had gone out of his way to make her distrust him, starting with kidnapping her at gunpoint, a crime she would make sure he rotted in prison for committing. He frightened her, too, but she was trying hard not to dwell on the frightening aspects of her situation—or of his personality.

He was silent, eerily so, and as unpredictable as a wounded animal. In one of the northern Colorado border towns, he'd twice pulled off the highway and into gas stations. Both times, after cruising the station at a crawl, he'd gotten back on the highway and driven on down the road. She didn't know what he was looking for, but he'd found Laramie, for what it was worth.

They stopped at a light on the outskirts of town. The streets were nearly empty and very quiet. The only sound she heard was his breathing, and it didn't sound good. She hazarded a quick glance in his direction.

The impression of a wounded animal came back to her. He was propped against his corner of the car with the shotgun wedged between the seat and the door. His breathing was ragged, his face pale under his beard stubble and his bruises. Nervous energy radiated off him as it did off a cat.

"Are you sick?" she asked.

Dark eyes, weary and determined, slanted her a brief look. Then he went back to his driving, silent as ever.

Dylan didn't have the strength to talk. It was taking everything he had to keep driving. He needed sleep, food, and medical attention. His pants were wet with his own blood, the front of his T-shirt saturated. He needed help, he needed a friend, and all he had was a woman he'd abducted with a twelve-gauge.

He spotted the lights of an all-night gas station and convenience store and headed toward them, careful to use his blinker and stay just under the speed limit. His last two attempts to get gas and supplies had been unsuccessful. A cop had been in the first station, standing toward the back of the store by the coffee machine. Dylan hadn't spotted the squad car, but he hadn't hung around to look for it either. The second station he'd tried just hadn't felt right, reason enough to leave.

He pulled into the Laramie station's parking lot at one end, taking his time in cruising by the front of the store. He made a slow turn at the other end of the lot and came back to park in front of the gas pump closest to the door of the store. He sat still for a minute, watching the clerk inside. The man was young, too young to know much about the kind of trouble Dylan was up to, and too young to know what to do even if he did figure it out. He was also in that gangly, awkward stage boys sometimes went through well into their twenties. Dylan figured he could take him without hurting him, if it came to that.

"Come on. You're going with me," he said to the woman beside him. He opened his door and set one booted foot on the pavement. With effort, he got his other foot out and slowly rose to a standing position, supporting himself with the car door.

She got out next to him, with a look on her face

he immediately recognized. She was ready to bolt, looking for any chance to lose him.

"Don't even think it," he said, angling the shotgun far enough away from his thigh for her to see it beneath his coat.

Johanna looked quickly from the gun to his eyes. "You have a strange way of trying to save someone's life," she said, carefully keeping her voice devoid of expression.

"I'll be more accommodating later. Right now I'm desperate." He drawled his words either from insolence or exhaustion. "Do you know how to pump gas?"

What she didn't know about the operation, he explained. She held the nozzle in the tank while he lounged against the car as if he didn't have the strength to stand up—a condition he proved when she was finished pumping the gas.

"Come here," he said when she had turned off the pump.

She thought they were close enough and was about to tell him so when he spoke again.

"Come here." His tone was deep and dark, definitely on the edge again.

Still, she hesitated.

He leveled the gun at her. *"Come here."*

She stepped closer, vowing he would pay dearly for every crime he committed against her. When she was next to him, he slid his right arm around her shoulders and rested the bulk of his weight against her. Her arm automatically circled his waist to keep them both from falling over, and a plan instantly formed in her mind.

The man was on the verge of collapse. All she had to do was wait for him to pass out, then make her escape. She could just walk away, get to the nearest police station, and the nightmare would be over. His body was trembling with the effort it took to walk into the store. His shirt and pants were damp with sweat. He felt hot and sticky. Lord, he felt like he was dying in her arms, and she was grateful.

She held him as they stumbled and limped down the aisles of the store, cleaning out the first-aid counter, buying prepared sandwiches, milk, juice, sport drink, the store's meager supply of fruit, instant coffee, and a sewing kit. In the personal-hygiene aisle, he asked her what she needed.

"That depends on how long you plan to hold me hostage," she told him with icy condemnation.

He met her gaze, unflinching. "One week."

"Then what?"

He pushed her forward. "Get what you need."

She literally had her hands full keeping him upright and retrieving the items he ordered her to put in their basket. She tried releasing her hold on him a couple of times in hopes he'd fall to the floor, maybe even unconscious, but each time he tightened his hold on her and pushed her onward.

In the candy aisle, he came to a stop. "Go ahead and get something."

She looked at him, confused. "Like what?"

At least a dozen different confections were within

easy reach. She didn't know if he wanted them all, or just a selection.

"I don't know," he said, with a brief, pained grimace. "Whatever you want. Something chocolate. You like chocolate."

"You don't know anything about what I like," she informed him coolly.

He actually grinned at that, an expression barely discernible from his grimace except for the teasing glint in his eyes. "I know you like chocolate, Miss Lane. Lots of chocolate. Preferably in gold boxes. But this"—he gestured at the rows of candy bars— "will have to do."

She did like chocolate, especially chocolate in gold boxes. Austin had kept her in constant supply—a fact Dylan Jones obviously knew. But that he considered her enough to act on that knowledge was what disconcerted her.

When she didn't make a move toward the candy, he did it for her, emptying a couple of the boxes into their cart.

"I'm trying to make this as pleasant as possible," he muttered, disconcerting her even more. As outlandish as his claim was, she believed him. Nothing in his manner was ingratiating. He didn't seem to give a damn whether she liked him or not, which ironically made her feel more secure. He wanted her to have the chocolate, simply because she liked chocolate.

Still, she wasn't going to let a few candy bars sway her determination. Her last hopes centered on signaling the night clerk for help. As they approached the counter Dylan drew her closer under his arm and nuzzled her neck. She instantly froze.

"Come on, honey." His words were definitely slurred, spoken in a sensuous timbre she would have thought impossible of him. His lips grazed her cheek in the same instant his gun grazed her thigh.

She lurched forward and began emptying their basket onto the counter, pulling stuff out, letting it pile up and fall over into the cigarette and candy displays crowded around the cash register. Chocolate or no, he didn't have any right to touch her like that.

The clerk gave them both a big, easy grin, his young face open, friendly, and freckled to match his rust-colored hair.

"Howdy, folks," he said, fishing a roll of first-aid tape out of the bubble-gum bowl. "Hope you found everything you wanted. These sandwiches were just brought in this morning, guaranteed fresh."

Neither Johanna nor Dylan commented on the sandwiches. Johanna because she had no intention of eating a smashed, day-old, convenience-store sandwich. Dylan because he didn't care how old or fresh the sandwiches were—he was going to relish every bite.

"You folks from around here?" the clerk asked, continuing his friendly chatter and ringing up their purchases.

"No," Dylan said, pressing against her as he dug in the pocket of his long overcoat. Johanna opened her mouth to speak, to say anything to keep the conversation going, but the clerk didn't need her help. He was talking again before she made her first sound.

"The weather's been pretty darn hot this summer. Hope you folks have some air-conditioning to keep you cool. Where you heading?"

"To bed," Dylan said, pulling his hand free of his pocket and sliding three boxes of condoms across the counter.

The conversation died an ignominious death. The clerk turned a bright shade of red, and his gaze skittered from the boxes to Johanna's breasts, to her thighs, back to her breasts, and finally to the cash register.

Johanna's face was red, too, but not from embarrassment. She hadn't seen him pick up the little boxes, but it took more than a condom, or even a dozen of them, to embarrass her. She was angry, plain and simple, and as soon as Dylan Jones was through saving her life and stuffing her full of cheap chocolate, she was going to nail his felonious hide to the wall.

Dylan paid cash for the supplies and nudged her leg with the shotgun. The condoms had done their job of shutting everybody up long enough for the clerk to finish his job, and none too soon. The muscles in his chest and shoulder ached and burned with the weight of the firearm. His head was pounding out a staccato beat of pain. His mouth was too dry to spit, and all he wanted to do was drop to his knees and the floor, preferably in a dead faint. Instead he was acting out a part he was all too familiar with, all too good at—the heavy. He nudged her again when she didn't move, pressing the barrel of the gun against her knee.

She slanted him a lethal look, her eyes narrowed in fury, and for a moment he thought she might call his bluff. He narrowed his own gaze in warning and pushed her harder.

"Move it, honey," he drawled. "We've got a *long, hard* night ahead of us."

The clerk grinned, and his gaze dropped once more to Johanna's breasts, irritating the hell out of Dylan. He said something crude to the kid, two succinct words meant to put him in his place. The kid's smile disappeared, and he got busy rearranging his candy displays.

Johanna leaned over the counter. "I want to use the phone," she said loud and clear, getting the clerk's attention. Dylan had to admire her for holding her ground, but she was also adding to his irritation. She'd called his bluff. Now he was going to call hers.

He took a second to concentrate his strength and take a breath, then he jerked her close, none too gently, and whispered in her ear. "If you drag the boy into this, he's going to get hurt."

Johanna stilled at the deadly intent in his voice. His grip tightened around her arm, a distinct contrast to the softness of his breath blowing across her skin. She shivered in an instinctive reaction.

"Let's move out," he murmured, and she let herself be half pushed, half pulled out of the store and back into the relentless heat of the night.

Dylan Jones had said he didn't want to hurt her.

He'd said he was trying to save her life. But he'd just made it damn clear that he would brook no interference from a stranger.

She slid into the sedan ahead of him and found her place in the middle of the seat, letting her head fall back. She didn't know if Austin had come to her apartment to hurt her or not, but she strongly suspected he had. It was unbearably naive to think otherwise. He hadn't talked to her in four months. Then, suddenly, the private company they'd put together was all over the newspapers and he needed to see her on a moment's notice.

The only thing that didn't fit, that didn't make sense, was the man next to her. He closed the door and let out a low sound, like a groan. Surprisingly, after praying for him to drop dead in the store, she felt the stirrings of compassion. She quickly squelched the absurd emotion. She wasn't in a position to be doling out compassion to a man who had kidnapped her, threatened her, and done his best to humiliate her.

"Why are you doing this?" she asked.

He shifted the car into drive and released the parking brake. The sedan eased forward.

"Are you working for somebody? What's in it for you?" She kept at it, demanding answers to her questions. "You owe me an explanation."

"Shut up . . . please," he said, his voice painfully tired. He checked in both directions for traffic before pulling onto the road.

Johanna leveled a glare at him he didn't see and stiffly crossed her arms in front of her chest. She didn't stop talking because he'd asked, but because she didn't want to waste her energy, or his. He hadn't had the grace to collapse in the store where she would have been safe. She didn't want him to do it behind the wheel of the car while she was in it.

She needn't have worried. He drove only a couple of miles before pulling into the parking lot of a brand-name highway motel. She didn't voice a single complaint when he dragged her inside to register. She had the routine down pat, and her other option had been a big roll of tape he'd shown her. Nor did she hesitate when he ordered her into room number seventy-two. They were in a motel, and she didn't have a doubt in her mind that she could outlast him in the consciousness department. From her observations, it was a miracle he was still on his feet.

The accommodations were clean and color-coordinated, neatly appointed. They were more than she had expected from him. From the looks of him, she would have expected him to choose a flea-bitten rat hole facing an alley somewhere.

She put the grocery bag on the desk while he checked the bathroom, his duffel bag gripped tightly in his fist. He took one quick look and turned back toward her.

"If you want to use the facilities, now is your chance. You can close the door, but if you lock it, I'll blow it off its hinges."

Ever the gentleman, she thought sarcastically, stepping around him on her way to the "facilities." She had immediately spotted the telephone in the room, and she'd had an overwhelming urge to call Henry. Touching base with her partner would give her a sense of security, and she was badly in need of that. Unlike her captor, Henry was civilized and brilliant. True, he was also slightly scatterbrained and nearly eccentric in his habits, but he was as dependable as the day was long, and he was a damn good lawyer. She needed a damn good lawyer to begin her case against Dylan Jones immediately. She was going to bury the bastard in warrants.

Dylan eased himself into a chair outside the bathroom and rested the shotgun across his knees, promising himself he'd get up in a minute. He had a lot to do before the comfort of sleep could be his. He closed his eyes for a moment and took three deep breaths. Each one hurt in a different way. God, he was tired.

Stifling a groan, he leaned sideways in the chair and dragged the grocery bag closer to him. He ripped the paper bag down the middle with one hand, spilling the contents over the desk. His first choice out of the pile was a quart of milk, something healthy and wholesome. In between long, gulping swallows, he devoured one of the sandwiches and three candy bars, hoping to give himself a sugar rush without making himself sick. Something about profuse bleeding always made him nauseous.

Next he downed four aspirin and three ibuprofen tablets, wondering why, out of all the bad guys he knew, he had to be the only one who didn't have a stash of illicit drugs to fall back on in an emergency—because he was certainly facing an emergency. His gaze dropped to the sewing kit for an instant before he looked away. Time enough for that later.

He grabbed the bottle of sport drink and twisted off the top. After drinking half of it, he set the bottle aside and checked his watch. He'd give her five more minutes.

She opened the door at his third knock and gave him a scathing once-over, one eyebrow lifted in haughty disdain.

He would have laughed if he'd had the strength.

"Right," he drawled, agreeing with every nasty, low-down thing she was thinking about him.

She started to sweep past him, but he blocked the door with the shotgun.

"You don't have to leave," he said. "All I need is a shower, and I'm not shy."

At first Johanna didn't understand, but as his meaning sank in, her cheeks flamed. He couldn't be serious.

Proving that he was damn serious, he sidestepped into the bathroom and slowly closed the door behind him. She heard the lock click into place.

"Let me out of here," she said, her tone low and a little unsteady.

He shook his head. "I'm going to need help."

"You can go to hell."

He shrugged out of his long, khaki overcoat, wincing in obvious pain.

"I am not bathing you," she warned him, taking a step back.

"No, you're not," he agreed. "But you're safer in here where I can keep an eye on you, and when I'm done, I'm going to need some help."

"Help yourself." She took another step backward and came up against the sink. An edge of fear skittered across her nerve endings.

His coat fell in a pile at his feet, and her gaze dropped down his body. He was soaked through, his black T-shirt clinging to lean, solid muscles and the flat, hard plane of his abdomen. His jeans rode low on his narrow hips and encased the length of his legs in soft black denim down to where they broke across his boots.

He moved to lean the gun against the wall, drawing her gaze back to the weapon and his arm. Cords of muscle slid smoothly under his skin, but it was the blue star tattooed halfway between his elbow and his wrist that riveted her attention. Her heart started pounding too fast as she stared at the indelible design marking his skin. She'd seen that tattoo before, exposed by the rolled sleeve of an impeccably white shirt—in Chicago.

Against her will, her gaze traveled back up the length of his torso and locked on his face. The light was very good in the bathroom, bright and sharp, delineating the curves of his cheekbones and the sharper angle of his jaw. She looked into his eyes and swallowed. Within those dark, feral depths was something she'd once felt too intensely ever to forget.

His hands went to his belt buckle, and Johanna's panic stirred to full flight. She knew who he was.

FOUR

Dylan knew the instant she recognized him. His hand stilled on his belt, and his gaze slipped away from hers. He wished she hadn't remembered.

A mocking voice inside his head called him a liar. He'd made a career out of being invisible, but some part of him liked to think that no matter how deep he went undercover, he was still Dylan Jones. He liked to think he wasn't the only person who say beyond the bad-guy surface to the good guy underneath. He liked to think that when a man bared his soul and nearly risked his life for a kiss, that the woman he'd risked it for would remember.

Well, she remembered all right. His gaze lifted as he finished with his buckle and pulled his belt free. Memories and stark disbelief were written all across her pretty, pale face, and it terrified her more than when she'd thought he was a stranger.

"*You*," she gasped, the word less than a whisper.

He swore silently, wondering what to do next.

After a second's hesitation he said, "You don't need to be so frightened. I'm with the FBI." At least he thought he was still with the FBI. It had been a while since he'd heard from anybody on the other side of the law, from anybody on the right side. He heard from the wrong side every hour of every day. He lived, breathed, and would probably die on the wrong side of the law. He'd accepted that fact weeks ago.

She slowly shook her head and backed farther away from him, wedging herself between the vanity and the bathtub. It was as good a place as any to his way of thinking.

"If you want to sit next to the sink, that's fine with me," he said, walking toward her, his boots making soft scraping sounds on the tile floor of the bathroom.

"I want to leave." She tried to move away, but there was no place left for her to go. He saw the panic come back into her eyes.

No doubt about it, he made a hell of a hero.

"Sit on the counter," he commanded her, his voice gruff, his patience at an end. He didn't have the time or the strength to coax her into anything, and in truth there was little need; he already had her cornered. He slowly reached for her hands, pinning her with a glare he hoped would keep her in her place. "If you fight me, you're the one who is going to get hurt, and I really don't want you to get hurt."

His words must have sunk in, because when he

finally closed his hand around her wrist, she didn't struggle. He made a loop with his belt and slipped it over both of her hands. He tightened the loop with a quick jerk, just quick enough and tight enough to remind her he was in charge.

"Dane . . ." The name whispered from her mouth, catching him unaware. He swore and his fingers trembled as he tied the belt back through itself. That was what she'd called him that night, *Dane*, the name she'd known him by.

"My name is Dylan Jones." And so help him God, he wanted it back.

"Dane Erickson," she said, her voice gaining a small measure of steadiness.

He didn't have the strength to argue with her. He bent down and got the tape out of his coat pocket. Within minutes he had her secured to the shower rod with a length of doubled and twisted cloth tape. She could continue to stand if she wanted to, but he'd given her enough slack to sit on the vanity, a kindness he doubted he would be thanked for providing.

Letting out a deep breath, he dropped the roll of tape to the floor and checked to make sure the shotgun was within easy reach of where he'd be in the shower. No one was going to get to her without going through him first.

Despite the smallness of the space they were in, he managed to ignore her presence as he struggled with getting out of his clothes. His boots went first, then his socks. Before he attempted the more difficult stuff, he leaned over the bathtub and started the water running.

Johanna stood stock-still in her prescribed area, stunned into silence by her realization and the situation. She'd been kidnapped by Austin's private bodyguard, Dane Erickson, and he was stripping in front of her, taking off his clothes piece by piece.

She swallowed hard, watching him and feeling complete mortification sink through every pore in her body. She had never expected to see him again, of all men, let alone see so much of him.

Color rose hotly in her cheeks. Dane Erickson had always been impeccably groomed, not like this man with his shaggy, raked-through hair, beard stubble, and bruised and cut face. But it was Dane, unbelievably. She had to stop him from taking his clothes off. She couldn't just stand there and watch him get naked—not him.

"You—you can't do this," she stammered. The immediacy of her current problem completely overrode her concerns over being kidnapped.

He ignored her and tugged his T-shirt out of his pants.

Desperate, she tried a new tack. "Whatever happened between you and Austin shouldn't involve me. I've got my own problems with him. He's not going to like that you've taken me."

"I don't give a damn what Austin doesn't like."

Despite his thoughtfulness with the chocolate, Johanna got the distinct impression he didn't give a damn what she didn't like either, because she certainly didn't like watching a man over whom she'd made a fool of herself undress.

And it was him. The smile had been a dead giveaway, but she'd been too frightened to put the feelings together with the right facts. Dylan Jones moved with the same controlled grace, the same efficiency, the same hint of wariness and threat that had set Dane apart from all the other men around Austin. Once, in an attempt to impress her, Austin had told her how much he'd had to pay to get Dane. The quiet, dangerous ones, he'd told her, always placed the highest price on their services. If they were also intelligent, the price went through the roof. The lesson, of course, hadn't really been about how good Dane was, but rather how powerful Austin was. He bought men like Dane; he could buy a woman like Johanna. At the same time she'd known he was wrong about her. Now she knew he'd also been wrong about Dane.

The man in front of her had obviously never been bought, not even at Austin's outrageous price. Groaning softly, he straightened, his hands sliding to the front of his pants. He slanted her a quick glance.

"I don't recommend watching," he said in a flat tone.

Horrified to have been caught staring, she squeezed her eyes shut. Lord help her. She'd really gone and done it this time, gotten herself kidnapped by a man who had a reason to think she might actually enjoy the experience. Logically she knew the work she'd done for Austin was the reason for her abduction. When she considered her abductor, though, she knew her imagination was also to blame. It and a wayward curiosity had led her into one regrettable indiscretion she was sure he hadn't forgotten. And if by some outside chance he had forgotten, her uncontrollable, blossoming sexual awareness of him was bound to remind him.

It wasn't a pleasant sexual awareness. Quite the contrary, it was particularly unpleasant and heavily laden with guilt. She was aware of every breath he was taking in the small room, every movement he made, and exactly where all those moves were taking him—naked into the shower.

The awful thing was that she'd imagined him naked at least a dozen times during her last weeks at Bridgeman, Inc. He had the kind of body that did that to a woman, made her imagine all sorts of things. None of the other female attorneys or secretaries had seemed to notice, at least not to the same degree, or so they'd said whenever Johanna had gotten up the nerve and nonchalance to mention Austin's newest bodyguard. A couple of the less observant women hadn't even known who she was talking about.

He did have a chameleon's talent for blending into his surroundings, for being inconspicuous. But Johanna had noticed him the first time he'd shown up next to her employer, and she had never been able to disconnect her awareness of him. The last time she'd seen him had been proof enough of an attraction that had gone too far.

She had analyzed the events of that night a hundred different ways and had never come up with a reason for his actions. She had come up with plenty of reasons for her own actions, and none of them showed her in a very good light.

"Desperate female attorney makes pass at willing bodyguard" was as close as she could get to the truth. Except in the end he hadn't been willing, and she'd never been completely satisfied that the pass had been hers.

She had been working late in Austin's office, checking a last, necessary contract for the next day, when he had walked in, as silently as always. She had often wondered how long he'd been watching her. Of course, knowing wouldn't have made any difference to what had happened.

He'd almost kissed her . . . almost, and she hadn't forgotten how good "almost" had felt.

She'd been exhausted from overwork and feeling too alone, too abandoned to the night. The last person she'd been prepared to deal with had been Dane Erickson. From the beginning, he had been intriguing, compelling, and too damn good looking, with his street toughness barely concealed by a veneer of sophistication, as if he'd just stepped into Austin's plush office from the wild side of town. . . .

Johanna leaned back in Austin's deluxe leather chair and stretched her feet up to rest on a corner of the teak desk. A sheaf of legal documents filled her lap. Fortunately, from what she'd seen so far, the papers were in order. Austin Bridgeman had taken to playing rather fast and loose with the law. She never knew what to expect from him anymore, which was why she had decided to leave. Looking over the contracts for him on such short notice was a final thank-you on her part for the opportunities he'd given her.

She perused the papers, rubbing the nape of her neck with one hand and yawning. She needed to exercise, or get a chiropractor, or a massage. All the tension in her life seemed to settle in her neck and shoulders. The muscles there were tighter than iron bars. Her mother thought she worked too hard and needed a husband and children. Her father thought she needed to come to work for Lane, Lane, and Sullivan, or give him a son-in-law for the firm, and her sister thought all she really needed was a lover. Lovers, she explained, were where husbands came from.

And vague language is where lawsuits come from, Johanna thought, drawing a line through a paragraph and making corrective notes in the margin. After another yawn, she propped her chin on her hand and continued reading.

Working less or working for her father—as much as she loved and admired him—were out of the question. She had followed in his footsteps, but she didn't want to step in exactly the same places. A love life didn't seem to be much in the running either, though she'd been thinking about it more than usual lately. Unfortunately the man she'd been thinking about was out of the question.

She flipped a page, a small smile curving her lips. She was definitely out of line in that area. Too many long days and an equal number of lonely nights had gone to her head. An enigmatic bodyguard with midnight-dark eyes, blond hair, and rare but sinfully suggestive smiles would give her whole family a collective heart attack. But then, her family and acceptable suitors had been her problem all along in finding a Mr. Right. Appropriately perfect men left her cold, and when she did find a man who warmed her imagination, he was totally inappropriate.

She had talked to a therapist about it once, asking the doctor if she thought it was some residual, latent, adolescent rebellion she hadn't worked through. Two sessions later there had been no definitive answer, but Johanna had come away from the therapy determined to put her family's matchmaking to a halt. That had left her with little to do except ignore the whole issue of her nonexistent love life.

Then Austin had hired a new bodyguard.

Her finger paused halfway down the page. She read the paragraph again, trying to concentrate. The man had been having that effect on her since the day he'd arrived, and no one could have been more inappropriate for a Chicago Lane than Dane Erickson. Unfortunately no one had ever appealed to her so strongly.

With effort, she finished the paragraph and moved on to the next one. Another yawn and her concentration wavered, shifting to a much more pleasant subject than the contract in her hand.

Dane Erickson was so serious most of the time, and so seriously fascinating. It was more than just his looks, though he exuded a sexual magnetism she found impossible to ignore. When he walked into a room, her awareness heightened, and she invariably found herself searching him out. He'd caught her staring at him more than once, much to her embarrassment. The brief but potent smiles he'd given her on those occasions had nearly been her undoing. She was supposed to be above such knee-weakening reactions.

He was safely off limits for reasons besides his occupation. Office romances were inevitably messy, disastrous affairs, and Austin had called him dangerous. That was part of his appeal, she was sure, but it was also reason enough for her to hold tight to her common sense. There would be no passionate fling between herself and Dane Erickson—no matter how many times the idea came to mind.

Sighing with exhaustion, she put her pencil down and rubbed the bridge of her nose. She did work too hard. It was time to go home.

By touching a panel on the desk, she was able to turn out all the lights in the office except for the desk lamp. She set the papers down and swiveled around in the chair to look out over the city. The view from Austin's office was magnificent, one of the many things she knew she would remember and sometimes miss.

She was heading to Boulder, Colorado, to a new partnership with an old friend, and Dane Erickson would remain a mystery. All for the best.

Damn, she thought. That's the way it always worked in her life. The job came first and fascinating men came last. Resigned to the inevitable, she turned the chair back to the desk.

"Miss Lane."

She jerked her head up, surprised to find the object of her fascination standing in the doorway. The contract papers slid out of her hand and across the desktop.

"Mr. Erickson." She managed to speak with difficulty, then quickly looked down and busied herself with the spilled papers. "I . . . uh . . . didn't think your work kept you at the office so late."

"I didn't think yours did either."

She sensed him stepping farther into the office, and a flush of excitement coursed its way through her system. Her face grew warm. Despite all of her common sense, she felt anticipation rise along the length of her body.

"I saw the lights," he continued. "I thought I should come up and check things out. I didn't expect to find you."

"I didn't expect to be found," she admitted with a slight laugh. "I should have been finished hours ago."

He was still coming closer, and she instinctively rose to her feet. He made her nervous in a dangerous way that she didn't dare explore. For the first time ever, they were alone in a room together, and the knowledge was having a dramatic effect on her.

She glanced up, but her gaze got no further than his mouth. She stared, overwhelmed by the possibilities of being alone with him, and as she stared he smiled. The slow curve of his mouth and the crease deepening in his cheek promised a devastating combination of mischief and thrills that she suddenly wasn't sure she could live without.

"I'll walk you to your car," he said, stopping next to the desk, closer than he'd ever been . . . close enough to touch.

"No. No," she stammered, gathering up her papers with both hands to keep herself from doing something rash and surely regrettable. "That won't be necessary. I'm in the executive parking garage. There's always somebody on duty down there."

"You'll be safer with me," he said. The conviction in his voice belied his smile and implied much more than a simple walk to the executive parking garage.

Her hands tightened on the papers, and against her better judgment she lifted her gaze to his and told him the truth. "I'm not so sure about that."

In the next second she knew the truth had been a mistake. He wasn't going to let it go as a slip of the tongue or a light flirtation. He had taken the truth to heart in all its meanings.

He stepped closer and lifted his hand to her waist, his smile fading. His touch alone would have been enough to surprise her, but he went much further than a touch. He held her gaze with his and grasped her blouse, already half-pulled from her skirt. He eased it free, both shocking and arousing her.

She'd never known a man whose initial move was to undress the woman he wanted. But then she'd never known a man like Dane Erickson. Her pulse raced when he slid his fingers under her blouse and caressed her waist. His hand was hot.

She looked down to where he touched her, seeing the darkness of his forearm against the white silk of her blouse. His shirt was white, too, neatly rolled up from the cuff, revealing a secret. A tattoo marked his skin halfway between his wrist and elbow, a pale blue star outlined in a deeper shade. She lifted her hand to his shoulder and felt the strength of his arm come alive under her fingertips as he drew her closer.

"Dane," she said softly, lifting her gaze back to his. . . .

She'd whispered his name, Johanna remembered, which had made her humiliation complete when he'd turned and walked away.

A flush of embarrassment coursed up her cheeks. She had definitely been attracted to Austin's enigmatic bodyguard, against all the rules of professional conduct, against every ounce of her common sense.

She heard his jeans drop to the bathroom floor, and the color in her face deepened. What common sense? she wondered. She obviously didn't have the sense God had given a goose, if the extent of her romantic fantasies consisted of herself and a hired bodyguard with criminal tendencies.

He groaned, and her eyes flew open. She just as quickly shut them again, her heart suddenly pounding. *My God, my God.* He was hurt. She'd seen blood, lots of it, staining his briefs and dried across his belly where he'd raised his T-shirt.

He swore, sounding thoroughly disgusted with something, and she heard the shower curtain being drawn aside with a swift jerk. The swearing increased when he entered the shower. She let her breath out on a trembling sigh and slowly opened her eyes, then opened them wider. A new wave of embarrassment washed through her from her toes to the top of her head.

Her captor had sorely miscalculated the position of the tape on the shower rod. The curtain didn't reach to the wall on her end of the bathtub. Other than closing her eyes or making herself incredibly uncomfortable by twisting her body in the other direction, there was no way for her not to see him and his struggle. He was still decently covered in his briefs and T-shirt, but she knew that condition wouldn't last long.

She watched, mesmerized, as he inched the T-shirt up his torso, careful of whatever wound had caused all the blood. His back was smoothly muscled, well defined, a slowly revealed line of sweat-sheened skin from waist to shoulder. She had touched him there once, she remembered again uneasily, laid her hand on his shoulder and felt the muscles bunch and slide beneath her fingers as he'd moved her closer.

He swore and swore again, softly and vehemently, as he pulled the shirt over his head. When it was off, he let it fall into the bathtub with a splash and leaned forward into the spray, looping his wrists over the shower head. A low, masculine groan rumbled up from his chest as he bent his head under the water and let it sluice off his hair and face.

He suddenly looked vulnerable and in dire need of protection, this man who was paid to protect. From the amount of pink reddening the water at his feet, she guessed his underwear was as stuck to his body with blood as his T-shirt had been. Therefore, logic told her it was a mere matter of time before he took those off too.

Less time than she'd thought, she realized, when he hooked one thumb into the side of his underwear and began pushing down. She should look away now. Prudence required it. Decency insisted. She ignored both.

Dylan felt her gaze the way he'd always felt it, like a hot touch on his skin. He'd realized his mistake the first time he'd moved the shower curtain. He could have cut her free and repositioned her, but like he'd said, he wasn't shy, and he would have bet a thousand dollars against her looking.

So he'd lost a figurative thousand dollars. Just looking at him wasn't likely to shock her, and she was unlikely and unable to do anything that might shock him. She could always look away, whereas his options were a damn sight narrower. He needed to get himself cleaned up and doctored, and he needed to do it before he fell asleep on his feet or passed out.

With his goals firmly in mind, he clung to the

shower head and doused himself with the little bottle of complimentary shampoo. He picked up the neatly wrapped bar of soap and used his teeth to rip the package open. He spat the paper out, and it fluttered to the bottom of the bathtub. Wincing, he ran the soap across his chest and down over his belly. He had a few more bruises than he'd thought, and a shallow cut under his right arm. His groin was fine. His butt was in pretty good shape, too, except for feeling flat as a pancake from two days of hard driving across the heartland.

Carefully reanchoring himself to the shower head with his left hand, he lifted his left leg and soaped his thigh and calf.

"Damn," he muttered, coming across another nick in his skin. That little bastard, Johnny, had managed some quick work with his knife.

Dylan found another cut on his right thigh. All his small pains had kind of melded together into one big ache. Now he knew what was where. The big cut, the deep slash on his chest, had maintained a personality all its own throughout the last two days.

Finished with his body inventory, which had included another cut low on his right shoulder, he ran a hand through his hair, shampooing and checking for damage at the same time. The inevitable bruises surfaced as lumps, nothing of concussion quality. He was pretty damn hardheaded.

He turned around to rinse the shampoo out of his hair. Then he remembered she was watching.

Squinting against the water running down his face,

he met her surprised gaze. Her hazel eyes were wide and startled from the fast trip they'd made up his body.

He grinned despite the effort it took. "We're gonna have a problem here, if you're not careful," he drawled.

Johanna was speechless, trapped on her end of the shower rod with a guilty blush streaking across her cheeks. When he turned back around, she dropped her head into the cradle of her arms and groaned softly.

Dylan heard the muffled sound and was surprised to find himself physically reacting. Who would have thought he could be stirred to arousal in his condition? His warning her about "problems" had been more along the lines of a joke or a hope. He wasn't the man of steel. Yet she'd made a soft sound, and he'd instantly equated it with a response he could draw out of her with his mouth on her body, anywhere on her body, though certain particular parts did come to mind.

In the seconds it had taken him to register her embarrassment and capitalize on it, he had noticed plenty about her anatomy. Silk T-shirts had a way of clinging all on their own. Adding steam and humidity made them wonderfully indecent. Her breasts were full and beautifully shaped, curved to fit the palm of a man's hand. Her bra was lace. Her damp skin shone like cream-colored satin.

He realized he was feeling better and better, a condition he would have thought impossible five minutes earlier. The woman was a tonic, her presence a soothing balm on his aches and pains.

A grin eased its way across his face. He had saved her life. She was alive because of him. He was winning.

FIVE

Johanna rubbed her wrists with her freed hands. The skin wasn't chafed or sore—he'd been too careful for that—but the action kept her from wringing her hands. She hadn't quite recovered from his shower—she doubted if she ever would—and now he was proposing something even more outrageous. She nodded as he explained what he wanted her to do, even though she had no intention of complying.

"I think three or four stitches ought to do it," he said, looking at her from under raised eyebrows, as if she were a child he was trying to convince to eat her vegetables.

She nodded again, all the while thinking she was an attorney, dammit, not a paramedic. Didn't he know that?

After his shower, he'd left the bathroom with a towel wrapped around his waist and returned dressed in a pair of dove-gray jeans and nothing else. He'd brought his duffel bag, all the first-aid supplies, and the sewing kit back in with him. He'd brushed his teeth, shaved, and combed his hair before releasing her, each action making him more of the man she remembered.

Dane Erickson, Dylan Jones, it didn't matter. He wanted her to do the impossible with the small package of needles and thread.

"I think if you just set your mind to it and do it fast and clean, it'll be a lot easier on both of us." He kept talking, his gaze shifting from her to the needle he was sterilizing, and she kept nodding.

"Leave yourself plenty of thread on each end to tie off. Make every stitch separate."

"Right." There was no way on earth she was going to stick a needle into his flesh. Her gaze drifted down his chest, past the cut slashed below his collarbone. He was beautiful, more so than she'd once imagined, all sleek muscles and golden skin. But there were signs of a hard life, nicks and bruises—and that awful knife wound. She couldn't do it.

"Don't worry about hurting me. I'm not going to scream or knock you over or anything." Dry laughter accompanied his statement.

"Okay." Her voice was bleak, her heart pounding an erratic rhythm.

"I don't suppose you have any penicillin on you? Or anesthetic?" He laughed again, a soft, gravelly sound she doubted he ever got beyond. She knew he was trying to relax her so she could do the job that needed doing. He was the one who was hurt, but she was the one shaking like a leaf.

"No. No anesthetic." She responded automatically, without any attempt to match his wry humor. She didn't have even the smallest smile to offer him.

He had kidnapped her, dragged her through the night with a gun at her head, and she hated him for that. He had embarrassed her beyond the ends of the earth during his shower, and she hated him for that. Then he'd gone and been brave and very matter-of-fact about what needed to be done to hold his body together, and he'd stirred her respect to life. He'd made her feel compassion, and she didn't know what to think. She remembered what he'd made her feel months ago, when he'd been Dane Erickson and she'd been safe behind her executive desk, and that frightened her. It was the only thing left that did frighten her. The night had been full of threats and violence from the instant he'd grabbed her, but there wasn't a mark on her. He'd told her twice he didn't want to hurt her, and he was a man who got what he wanted. He wasn't going to hurt her, not with his hands, or the shotgun, or any of the other myriad weapons he had stashed in his duffel bag along with his clothes.

"Ready?" he asked, pulling a length of thread through his antibiotic-cream-smeared fingers.

"No," she said softly, her jaw tightening, her emotions suddenly getting away from her. "Damn you, I am not ready. You can't make me do this."

He lifted his head, and his gaze flicked over to where he'd laid the shotgun on the vanity.

"No," she repeated, aware of the action and the subtle meaning behind it. "You don't scare me."

"I could." He let his gaze drift back to her. The threat was clear in the mahogany depths of his eyes.

Johanna knew she was playing with fire. Austin had called Dane quiet and dangerous, and both descriptions were true. But an attorney wasn't much use to anyone if she let herself be pushed around. She faced him squarely, her chin lifted.

Dylan noted the obstinancy tightening her soft lips, the stiffness of her shoulders, and he lowered his eyes, letting her win. He wasn't going to shoot her, and she'd finally figured it out. But he still needed her help. He was as tough as the next guy, tougher than some, maybe tougher than most, but he'd be damned if he thought he could sew himself up.

"Please," he said. The word came out rough and foreign sounding, and he realized it had been a long time since he'd asked anyone for anything. Within seconds, he knew it hadn't been long enough.

A long, tense silence ensued, stretching between them and filling up the small space. Dylan was sorry he'd asked. Damn sorry. He didn't mind looking like a mean son of a bitch, but he hated looking like a fool.

"Get out," he said under his breath, turning away from her.

He busied himself with his preparations, waiting for her to leave, not really caring how far she went. He'd saved her life once, and once was more than he'd thought he could pull off. She'd seen Austin and his goons. She was smart enough to go to the police.

Maybe.

Maybe not.

Dammit. Even if she went to the police, they couldn't protect her, not the way he could. She wouldn't last forty-eight hours without Austin picking up her trail, and once he did that, she wouldn't last another two.

He turned to retract his command and caught her rising from where she'd sat on the edge of the bathtub. As she reached toward the vanity he grabbed her wrist. Their eyes met, and he finished pulling her to her feet.

"I've changed my mind," he said.

"So have I," she countered, her voice no less angry than it had been before. She tugged on her wrist.

He held her just long enough to reestablish his authority.

Agreeing in silence, he sat on the counter next to the sink and Johanna took the needle in hand. She knew what she had to do . . . sort of.

She looked at his chest and the neat slice arced between collarbone and breast. Logically thinking about stitching him up and actually doing it were going to be two completely different experiences. That was her first realization. The second was how soft his skin was beneath her fingers. She touched him lightly with her fingertips, but the softness and warmth of him registered as if she'd caressed him with her open palm.

Damn. Of all the men who worked for Austin, why did he have to be the one to be a part of her personal crisis?

She stepped away from him and averted her eyes. "Where are the scissors? I don't want to start this until I have the scissors handy."

"Here." He pointed them out, lying next to the sterile bandages and the extra tubes of antibiotic cream.

"Fine," she muttered under her breath, returning to her station in front of him. His knees were on either side of her hips, not touching her, but noticeably present. Sewing someone up was close work. There was no getting around the need to touch him, the need for sharing the same intimate space.

She steeled herself to do the impossible, willing herself not to falter. Despite all he'd done to her, she didn't want to hurt him. She didn't want her cowardice, inexperience, or ineptitude to cause him more pain. She expected it to be difficult to get the needle through his skin.

It was.

Dylan swore, one harsh word. She pushed harder, forcing the needle through, and his cursing became a softly spoken, endless litany. He gritted his teeth against the pain and the lure of unconsciousness. If he passed out, she'd be out the door in a minute. The game would be lost and they both would die.

The thread slipped through his skin less painfully. His relief was a tangible entity flooding his senses.

"You smell the same," he said roughly, speaking the first thought that came into his mind, needing to hear the sound of his own voice to keep holding on.

Her concentration faltered for a moment, showing

in the hesitation of her hands before she tied off the stitch.

"Your perfume," he explained. After just one suture, he didn't think this was such a great idea. Sweat had broken out on his brow, his muscles were twitching and jumping, but he liked having her close. It helped fight off the weakness trying to engulf him. "I could always tell when you'd been in Austin's office. Your scent would be there for a long time after you left, real subtle, but I could always tell. It used to drive me crazy."

She raised the needle for the second stitch, but he wasn't ready. He grabbed her wrist again when she would have pierced his skin.

"Don't." There was an edge to his voice.

"I have to," she whispered, not sounding any surer than he felt.

They made a fine pair, he thought, captor and captive when they should have been lovers. He'd wanted everything from her except this, to use the best of his least redeeming skills against her, to trap her into sharing a closeness she'd once been willing to give.

"I always wondered what I'd missed," he said, his voice husky with a yearning he had no right to feel.

Her hazel eyes flicked up to meet his. "You were at enough of those meetings to know you didn't miss anything."

She'd misunderstood, which was for the best. This wasn't the time to tell her how many nights he'd lain awake thinking about how it had felt to caress her skin, to have her mouth nearly touching his. His relationship to her had been irrevocably changed from seduction to survival, yet he wasn't ready to relinquish his memories to the pain awaiting him.

"I was at enough of them to know Austin wanted to take you to bed. You were safe, you know. I never would have let him get closer than you were comfortable with."

She lowered her lashes. "Not even Austin Bridgeman always gets what he wants."

"What about you, counselor?" he asked, still holding her wrist.

"If I always got what I wanted, I wouldn't be here, doing this. I'd be safe at home."

"Alone? Or with someone?" He'd thought about the possibility. She hadn't been seeing anyone in Chicago. But she'd left Chicago four months ago.

Johanna ignored his question and prayed he would release her, because she could not ignore the man. Being the cause of his pain had forced open the gates of her compassion, and with that damnable compassion had come all the other feelings she hadn't wanted to surface.

Her gaze dropped to his lap, and her cheeks colored. Since his shower, she knew what he looked like there. She remembered the night he'd held her and how much she had wanted him. She remembered the emptiness he'd left behind when he'd turned and walked out of Austin's office, and the shame she'd felt for offering him something he hadn't wanted. In a quiet, surprising moment, desire had made a fool out of her with a man who should have remained a stranger.

"I'm sorry," he said, letting go of her wrist. "That's none of my business."

She readied herself to take the second stitch, then couldn't do it. "You've been hurt before," she said, stalling with the needle in her hand.

He followed her gaze to his shoulder. "I was shot. Tore some of the muscle, but it healed okay."

"Maybe you need a new line of work."

He flashed her a quick, surprising grin. "Right," he drawled, filling the word with irony and sarcasm.

"I'm going to do this again," she said softly, holding his gaze. She lifted the needle, and his grin disappeared as quickly as it had come. He nodded.

She tried not to hear the hiss of his indrawn breath, or see the involuntary trembling of his muscles. At the end of the second suture, he took her hand in his again.

"You need to give me a minute." His voice was a grating whisper between ragged breaths.

She hurt for him, hurt for him so badly. The last stitch had visibly paled him. The feathery lines at the corners of his eyes had deepened into creases. His lashes had lowered, half concealing those eyes, and his mouth was tight with strain, but she had to continue. "I don't want to drag this out any more than you do."

"I still need a minute, counselor." Dylan didn't let go of her hand, but held it tighter, slipping her fingers around into his palm. Her skin was so soft, a pleasure to feel against his. More than her softness, though, he needed her strength. He was dizzy, and his nausea had returned.

He closed his eyes and felt her other hand come to rest on his forehead.

"You're hot," she said, pressing her palm and fingers across his brow. "Let me get you some aspirin."

"I already took four, and three of the other."

"How did you let this happen to you?" The tone of her voice and the gentleness of her hand told him it wasn't an idle question.

He slowly opened his eyes and looked at her, just looked at her. She was gut-wrenchingly beautiful, everything he'd dreamed about for weeks and months, well worth the price he'd paid to save her life. Maybe the only thing worth the price he would pay in the end.

Johanna held his gaze as long as she could without succumbing totally to the longing she saw in his eyes. He was dangerous, and the tenderness in his touch had no place in the grim reality of their situation. He was still a stranger, she told herself, a hardened, battle-weary stranger, with a streak of ruthlessness that had made her the victim of a crime . . . and had probably saved her life.

"I'm only going to do this one more time," she promised, and felt a lump of regret settle in her throat as he closed his eyes in silent acceptance. She would hurt him once again, then no more.

When she finished her third and final stitch, she set the needle and thread aside and picked up the tube of antibiotic medication. Her hand started shaking as she squeezed the cream across the wound. What she'd done to him looked awful, and he still hadn't opened his eyes. A doctor would have used at least twice as many stitches. The scar would be jagged and wide, worse than necessary.

She reminded herself that she'd only done what he'd asked, but she wished someone else had done it. Despite her trembling hands, she taped a layer of sterile bandages over the wound with methodical efficiency.

"Don't get this wet again," she said, running nervous fingers over the edge of the tape, pressing it into place. "You should never have taken a shower. A doctor should look at this, but don't mention my name. I'd be arrested for practicing medicine without a license."

His strained voice spoke above her. "You did a good job."

She looked up quickly, worried by the weakness she heard. If he passed out, she would have to get him to a hospital. There was no telling what kind of massive infection might set in from her sewing him together like a ripped shirt. She wouldn't have his death on her hands, or on her conscience.

"A damn good job," he repeated, his voice gaining a surprising measure of strength and relieving her uppermost worry.

"I'm an attorney," she said, deliberately reminding both him and herself of who she was, and subtly implying that attorneys always did good jobs, especially if the attorney was Johanna Lane. It took a lot of brazenness on her part; she felt like a butcher. Now that the worst had passed, though, she needed to regain her distance and forget her lapse into compassion and his lapse into best-forgotten confessions. She returned her attention to putting away the first-aid supplies.

"Austin Bridgeman's private attorney," he said, carefully pushing himself off the vanity to stand beside her, proving to her that she'd underestimated his strength. It was something she'd be wise not to do again.

He was too close in the confined space. His bared chest was less than a hand's length away. His jeans fit him too well around his narrow hips. His belly was lean and ridged, with a dark taper of hair arrowing beneath his pants. She took a step away from him.

"Ex-attorney," she said on a short breath, putting the unused bandages back in their box. "I haven't worked for Bridgeman in four months."

"I remember when you left," he said as he handed her a bandage she'd missed. "I remember exactly when you left."

So did she, and her face warmed again. He couldn't have made his meaning more clear, or his lapse back into intimacy more apparent.

Dylan watched the color rise in her cheeks and felt a sense of victory. He'd made her remember what he'd never forgotten—the last time he'd seen her in Austin's office. . . .

He watched her from the darkened doorway. He watched the play of light along her legs and his gut tightened. She was leaving. He'd known for a week, and his first reaction of relief had been giving way to regret ever since.

Things were going to come down hard at Bridgeman, Inc. before the year was out. If she stayed, she'd be dragged down too. But when she left, he wouldn't see her again. The realization hurt in a way he was unused to feeling. A few women had come and gone in his life. He didn't know why he felt a need to hold on to one he'd never had—except she was gorgeous, vulnerable, and more in need of a friend like him than she knew. She was clean, but Austin wasn't, and the longer she associated with him, the dirtier she was going to get. He didn't want that to happen to her.

He noted the tiredness around her eyes and the uncharacteristically rumpled silk blouse only half tucked into her skirt. He wished he could ease some of the burden she carried, but Johanna Lane was prohibited territory—despite the shy, heated glances he'd intercepted from her. He was on a case, working under an alias, and however attracted she was to him, she was also smart enough to stay away. He was trouble, and she knew it. He'd seen her make the decision to look but not touch every time he caught her eye.

She pushed a silken fall of honey-blond hair back off her face, and suddenly he wondered what it would take to make her change her mind. Prohibited or not, he wanted her to touch him.

She turned the chair back toward the desk then, and he stepped farther into the room.

"Miss Lane."

Startled eyes met his across the expanse of plush carpet and expensive furniture. It took only a few seconds for her to recognize him, and her surprise turned into a subtle excitement he felt even at fifteen feet.

"Mr. Erickson," she said, lowering her gaze and fiddling with the papers on the desk. "You're working late."

"So are you." He walked deeper into the room, closer to the pool of soft light surrounding the desk and her. "I saw the lights, but I didn't expect to find you."

She laughed, a gently self-deprecating sound, and slanted him a quick glance. "I should have been gone hours ago."

"I'll walk you to your car," he said, continuing across the room and stopping at the desk. He was close, closer than he'd ever been. Close enough to touch.

"That won't be necessary," she said, gathering up her papers. "I'm in the executive parking garage."

"You'll be safer with me." He wasn't going to let her leave alone. The opportunity was too ripe. He'd waited too long.

She slowly lifted her lashes to meet his eyes, and he felt anticipation build inside him.

"I'm not so sure about that," she said softly.

She was right, but Dylan had never expected to hear her admit it. He let the silence lengthen, telling himself he was a fool—but he couldn't resist. With the barest movement of his hand, he reached to her waist and pulled out the rest of her white silk blouse.

The material cascaded into his fingers, feeling rich and soft, and warm from her body.

He held her gaze with his own, gauging her response in the faint mask of color spreading across her face. He heard her breath grow shallow. She wet her lips, and his groin tightened. It had been so easy to make her change her mind. It had taken nothing at all.

Her acceptance of his touch was a warm seduction to a heart that had been living outside the boundaries of truth for longer than he cared to remember. He grazed his fingers across the silky skin of her waist and forced himself to go no farther.

He wanted her with an ache he could feel pounding through his veins with every pulse beat. Every moment she allowed him to touch her was proof that she wanted him too. But he was a force of destruction.

His gaze slipped to her lips, and temptation made his mouth go dry. He was in over his head, way over his head, and if he didn't leave, he was going to drown in the hot sweetness of her.

"Dane . . ." she whispered, wanting him—but wanting the wrong man.

He closed his eyes and cursed softly, then, with an iron will, he turned and walked away. . . .

His memories did him no good. She was alone with him now and he was farther away than ever from what he wanted.

"How long have you been with the FBI?" she

asked, as if she, too, realized that what they might have had was now out of reach.

"Twelve years."

"Do you have any identification?"

A short, damning silence preceded his reply. "I left my badge in my other pants."

Johanna set the antibiotic cream aside and picked up the first-aid tape. She'd known he was lying about the FBI. He was exactly what she'd thought he was and nothing more. Her hands started shaking again.

"What do you want with me?" she asked. "What does Austin want?"

"Austin wants you dead."

She lowered her chin to her chest. What he said was impossible, unthinkable, yet she knew he was telling her the truth.

"And you?"

"I want you alive."

It didn't make sense.

She looked up and met his intense gaze in the mirror. He was watching her, waiting for her response. Now that he was clean and shaved, it was easy to remember why she had found him so attractive, so dangerously attractive. His face had a mischievous appeal, despite the deadly serious type of mischief he instigated. He had never made her uneasy like some of Austin's other bodyguards. No, the way he had made her uneasy was very private and exclusive—and he was still doing it. She had to be crazy.

"Does Austin know you've betrayed him?" she asked.

"I left him a message in Lincoln, Nebraska," he said coolly.

"Will he kill you too?"

"As soon as he gets his hands on me."

"What happens to me then?" She didn't mean to sound entirely self-centered, but her own survival was at the top of her priority list.

"I hope to have you someplace safe by then."

"Where?"

"I don't know yet."

She didn't like his answers. She didn't like his methods. A trembling sigh escaped her as she covered her face with her hands and lowered her chin back to her chest. She was doomed.

"You have to let me go. You have to. It's the only chance I've got, if I can get to the police."

"No." The single word was succinct.

"Why not?" she demanded, turning on him, her anger flaring to life.

His eyes hardened. His explanation was short, to the point, and delivered without apology or room for debate.

"Because any information the police have, Austin can get. Because if you walk into a station at two A.M., you'll be dead before dawn. Do you understand me?" He paused and pinned her with a glare so damn serious, it literally made her tremble. "I hope to hell you do, because whether you want to believe it or not, Miss Lane, I'm the best chance you've got of getting out of this alive."

SIX

She hated him. He was a despicable, unprincipled, criminal lout. He was a man without honor or conscience, and he was paranoid. There was plenty of proof for that assessment. All she had to do was look at the motel's furniture. He'd shoved one of the bed frames up against the door, then had angled the mattress over the window, propped up by a chair. He was mean and cruel and thoughtless, and he was crazy if he thought she was going to let him tie her up again.

"No," she said, her hands tightening into fists at her sides. She backed farther into the bedroom, widening the space between her and the belt coiled in his broad hands.

"It's for your own protection," he said calmly, following her with an easy, measured tread.

"Go to hell."

"I need to get some sleep. I can't do that if you're

up and wandering around, or up and wandering out of here."

"Then I guess you'll have to stay awake." Damn the man. She had put stitches in his skin, suffered along with him through every single stab of the needle, and he thanked her by tying her up again? Over her dead body.

"Impossible. I'm running on empty." He stopped at the edge of the bed and faced her, and as quickly as that, she was trapped once again. There was nowhere left to run in the room.

"That's your problem." To hell with compassion and empathy, she thought. She'd be damned if she let him tie her up. He did look like he was running on empty. He couldn't last too much longer.

"My problems are your problems," he said. "Or more to the point, your problems are my problems." He quickly and efficiently made a loop out of his belt.

"They don't have to be," she said, growing terse as the situation grew desperate. "You can't possibly know what Austin wants, and I do."

"Austin wants you dead. That's all he wants. Don't fool yourself into thinking you can barter with him. When you signed your name to Morrow Warner, you signed your own death warrant."

She blanched, and her heart skipped a beat. He'd said the damning words no one was supposed to know. "How do you know about Morrow Warner?"

"I looked." He shrugged, a tired lift of his left shoulder. "Every night you and Austin worked late,

I went back and looked over your work. If you think about it, you might remember that I was always the one on duty those nights. Or you might not remember. My job was to be inconspicuous."

"I remember," she said. She remembered too well, watching him out of the corner of her eye and feeling something she shouldn't have felt. "What you did was unconscionable and—and against the law. Those files were confidential."

His eyes narrowed for a moment in disbelief, then his lips curved into a sardonic smile. "Don't you ever forget you're a lawyer?"

"Austin could have fired you for looking at those papers," she said, lifting her chin to support her claim even as she realized how silly and empty her threat sounded.

"Austin Bridgeman is going to kill me, Miss Lane," he said dryly, all traces of his smile fading from his face. "And if I'm not as good as I think I am, he's going to kill you too. Then it won't matter which one of us knows what. You got yourself in good and deep by putting together Austin's little secret company, and now the piper wants his due without your interference." He lifted his hand and pointed behind her. "Get on the bed and lie down."

"I will not."

Dylan's jaw clenched in reaction to her prissy, holier-than-thou refusal. He heard his teeth grind together and felt muscles tighten in his face. Damn the woman. Didn't she know he could break her in five places and not even work up a sweat?

She had been his sole fantasy for six long, frustrating months, but he was beginning to think he'd been fantasizing about the wrong woman. Elegant Miss Johanna Lane, with her silk dresses and silk-clad legs, wasn't supposed to be scrappy. He had instinctively known it would be harder on him if or when she remembered him, but he was only beginning to figure out why. He'd thought it would be because of the night they had gotten so close to a kiss; he could still remember the sweet pressure of her body pressed up against his—because he wouldn't have left her with only a kiss. He would have had all of her. In his dreams he'd had her more than once. He had thought the memories of all that sexual heat would make it more difficult for him to remember he had a job to do, more difficult for him to remember that the end of his life was a damn poor time to get involved with a woman.

What he hadn't counted on was the elegant Miss Johanna Lane having steel in her backbone, for there being an edge to all the softness he'd seen and all the softness he'd visualized. Lawyers were supposed to be tough on paper and tough with words. But Johanna had made fists out of her expensively manicured hands, and he thought there was the chance she might use them.

Somewhere between the gas station and the bathroom, he'd started losing control of the situation. He'd lost completely the moment she recognized him. He needed to turn the tables around and get her back on unstable ground, and as long as she had thoughts about going to the police, he had to restrain her.

He started turning the tables by lowering his gaze from her wide eyes to her breasts. He deliberately stared, watching the slow increase in the rise and fall of her peach silk T-shirt, hoping to unnerve her before she had him on his knees, begging. She had beautiful breasts, and he could still see the lace of her bra. The image left itself open to a lot of wild imaginings.

He lifted his gaze back to her eyes and took a step forward, coiling the belt in his hands, remembering what he was about. Then he lowered his lashes and let his gaze sweep down the length of her body, with lingering moments on the curve of her hips and the juncture of her thighs. Her jeans fit her like a second skin without looking the least bit forced or strained. She was sleek and lovely, utterly female, and he was suddenly willing to risk everything to get closer to her, to feel her heat and hear her sigh.

Forgetting the belt and the job at hand, he took another step, much against the insistent clamorings of his common sense, which was telling him he was the one losing his balance. He couldn't deny that deep down inside, past the veneer of civilization and anyone's code of honor, there was a part of him that had saved her life only to make her his.

Johanna took a half step back, the only half step there was to take. The room was growing warmer, the tension rising, and he'd done it all with a glance of his midnight-dark eyes, a long, heated, suggestive glance that had visually traced her body and left her feeling touched.

"I think we should compromise," she said hurriedly, feeling the bed press against the backs of her knees.

"Compromise?"

"Negotiate."

"With what?" he asked, his voice a wary mix of confidence and sin-ridden hope.

She wet her dry lips with the tip of her tongue. He still wanted her. None of the attraction they'd felt had been forgotten, and it was all coming back to life under circumstances so wildly inappropriate as to be laughable, if they weren't so dangerous.

The man had guns—his ever-present shotgun, two or three handguns, and possibly a grenade or two in his duffel bag. She hadn't gotten a real close look, but she'd seen enough to realize he was a traveling arsenal.

When she had known him before as her boss's bodyguard, he had been physically attractive, mysteriously sexual, unfailingly polite—except for once—and he had been absolutely prohibited.

Now he was her ex-boss's enemy, anything but polite, and too damn close for comfort. Unfortunately he was still physically attractive and mysteriously sexual. She knew she needed her head examined, and the look in his eyes told her that he'd be willing to go along with any kind of personal examination she might care to come up with, but her intellectual parts wouldn't be his first choice for a starting place.

"Money," she said, more to break the increasingly uncomfortable silence than to make an offer—though she would be eternally grateful if he would take money to let her go. She needed to get away from him. He was half-naked and barefoot and they were alone, and all she could think about was the way he breathed and how his skin had felt when she had touched him. She tried to remember that he was the bad guy, that he had always been the bad guy, but her whole consciousness seemed to revolve around him being just a man and her being just a woman.

Dylan slowly shook his head. "I don't want your money, Miss Lane." He wanted her. But just like that other night, he knew he wasn't going to get her. He wondered what in the hell he'd ever done to deserve wanting this one woman he couldn't have. He had been far more physically intimate with other women without enduring a tenth of the frustration and longing he felt for Johanna Lane.

He narrowed the distance between them, taking the final step, until he could feel her breath upon his bare skin and watch her eyes darken to a deeper brown shot through with gold and green. He had kidnapped her. By any measure of morality, even his, she was as much forbidden fruit now as she'd been six months ago.

But he wanted a taste. Just one taste.

"Don't," she murmured, standing stock-still in front of him, barely daring to breathe, not daring to meet his eyes.

His hand touched her waist and slid to the small

of her back, and he felt the quickness of her indrawn breath. He brushed his mouth across the top of her cheek, warming her skin, and waited for her to say no again. She trembled in silence.

He lowered his mouth closer to hers. She turned away, and her voice accused him in ragged, breathless tones.

"Is this what you brought me here for? To . . . to abuse me?"

A pained smile briefly curved his mouth. "Is that what you were thinking every time I caught you checking me out?" he asked, letting a moment pass before he lifted his head. "That I was the kind of guy who would abuse you? Or were you thinking something else, Miss Lane?"

She'd been thinking something else, Johanna thought, and he damn well knew it. She wouldn't give him the satisfaction of an answer, though, not now, not in this place. She hardly dared to breathe for fear of increasing their contact or setting him off.

"You're right," he said, sounding defeated as he withdrew a few inches. "We'll both be better off if I never kiss you." His hands fell to her wrists and pulled them together, snaring them in the coils of his belt.

It took her a moment to realize what he'd done, but with realization came fury. She jerked her hands back, too late to free herself.

"You . . . you *bastard*!" She struggled, fighting the bindings in a losing battle. His greater strength won out with a judicious use of pressure and leverage.

"I'm worse than that, Miss Lane," he said, calm-

ly slipping the belt back through itself in the final
knot.

"*Liar.*"

"Now you're getting closer to my true nature," he
said, mocking her fury with infuriating composure.

An inarticulate screech of rage lodged in her
throat.

Trussed, Johanna thought. No, she amended.
Trussed meant tight and her bindings of belt and
tape were quite generous. She could move, she just
couldn't move away. From him.

Hobbled was a better word. Hobbled and humili-
ated. Humiliation seemed to be his particular talent.
He wasn't bad at hobbling either.

Groaning sleepily, he rolled over to face the wall,
and half of her went with him—her left arm and her
left leg to be precise. Her right hand was tied to the
bedpost.

"How in the hell," she muttered quietly, "am I
supposed to get any sleep with you dragging me all
over the bed?"

"And how in the hell," he muttered back, not
nearly so quietly, "am I supposed to get any sleep
with you talking all night long?"

"Let me go."

"Shut up."

"Bastard."

Dylan groaned in frustration. She was torturing
him, deliberately trying to drive him over the edge of

sanity. Every time he came close to slipping into the blessed nothingness of sleep, she started talking. She had already given him a rundown of his deplorable legal position as a felon. In her esteemed estimation, nothing short of life imprisonment would atone for his crimes against society, and most particularly for his crimes against her.

She had a thousand little comments tucked inside her smart, pretty head, a thousand little complaints, and he wasn't going to get any sleep until she'd voiced every one of them—or until he gagged her.

It was a thought, seductive in its simplicity. A washcloth. A strip of sheet. A double overhand knot. Blessed silence.

He groaned again, softer, more painfully. He didn't have enough strength left to gag her. He'd hit the wall. He hurt again. The respite allowed him by the sandwich and his shower was gone. The last vestiges of his energy had been stripped away.

"My partner, Henry Wayland—"

Dylan snorted a curse into the bedspread. God, how he hated her my-partner-Henry-Wayland.

"—is widely known for his belief in victims' rights. We'll demand restitution, and we'll get it. You can rest assured, Mr. Jones, that your assets are all but gone, all but mine."

"Mustang," he mumbled.

"What?"

"My Mustang. That's all there is and you're welcome to it."

He waited for her comeback, but she said nothing.

He had his coveted silence, *thank God*. All he'd had to do was give her his car.

He consciously relaxed his shoulders and let out a long, deep breath. Lazy dark tendrils of sleep began a slow spiral inside his head, beckoning him, promising him blessed oblivion. He drifted in their wake, floating ever downward, descending further and further into the welcoming abyss of—

"I can't believe that with what Austin was paying you, all you've managed to accumulate in assets is a car."

The tendrils of sleep fled before her snide, judgmental voice. His body instantly tensed to its more familiar alertness.

"It's a Shelby, a classic," he finally said.

"Oh."

The silence came again, but he didn't trust it. He didn't trust her. She was lying in wait for him—much as he'd lain in wait for her in her apartment hallway.

His first pang of guilt hit him. That was the trouble with his line of work: It was damn hard to do someone a favor and be nice about it. The stakes were always too high.

In lieu of the apology he wasn't willing to give, he swore silently to himself and *prayed* she was done for the night. His chest was burning, his head ached, his body hurt, and his eyes were gritty with the need for sleep. He couldn't take much more.

SEVEN

Johanna blinked sleepily at the light seeping in at the top of the drapes. She felt languorously alive and smiled, stretching her body into the unaccustomed pleasure of waking. Most mornings felt plain and predictable, but not this morning. A delicious, heavy thrill tingled through her; an inexplicable excitement filled the air. She yawned and stretched her arms—and found the limits of her tethers.

The night came back to her in a flash, and her eyes flew open to find Dylan Jones draped across her body. Her languor disappeared in a wave of anger and self-reproach. Where was her fortitude? Where were her survival instincts? And what in the hell did he think he was getting away with this time?

She wasn't supposed to have fallen asleep. She'd assured herself it would be impossible given the circumstances. But sleep she had, and well, if the enemy's incursions were any indication. His leg was lying casually and comfortably over her left calf and thigh with her knee cupped in the back of his. His pelvis was snug against her hip, and his hand was snug between her legs—quite snug. She could only imagine what kind of lewd mind it took to direct a sleeping man's subconscious to fondle a woman in her most private places.

Given half a chance, she would have shot him for all the horror and humiliation he'd put her through, and now this final, excruciating embarrassment of being groped in her sleep. But her one hand was still tied to the bedpost and her other was pinned with his against his rock-hard abdomen, alternately touching and not touching him as his muscles moved gently with his breath.

His breath . . . dear Lord. His breath played teasingly across the sensitive skin at her nape where he'd buried his head in the crook of her shoulder. He was all over her, pressed on top of her, touching her where he'd only dared to look before. She had to get away from him before anything else awful happened.

She cringed at the memory of the previous night and grew even angrier with herself. How in the world had she ever let herself fall asleep? And how in the world was she going to get away from him?

He had the guns, and that damn roll of tape he was always so eager to tie her up with. Her gaze inadvertently slid over the broad shoulder resting below her chin and followed the curved lines of muscle down his arm. He was strong, she admitted, but she was smart—smart enough to elude Austin without Dylan Jones's dubious help. She could lay low, follow the newspapers, wait for Austin to get arrested. . . .

She could wait forever for Austin to get arrested, she thought in dismay. There lay the truth of the matter. She had done a good job for Austin Bridgeman, maybe too good.

Dylan groaned softly and shifted in his sleep, and she felt the slow contraction and relaxation of each of his muscles like a heat wave caressing the length of her body. Her throat went dry, and she tried to remain perfectly still, perfectly blasé, while her senses ran amok.

She was in trouble, the kind of trouble she was famous for avoiding. Johanna Lane did not go around getting herself entangled with men, any kind of men, either emotionally or physically. She had never bought in to her older sister's theory of "It's a man's world, so get a man and get ahead," a theory her mother had raised to a high philosophy of woman as wife, mother, helpmeet, hostess, and slave to an autocratic if benign potentate, namely Johanna's father, the most renowned trial lawyer in the state of Illinois.

Johanna was different. Johanna was smart. Johanna was going to be like good old Dad. But Lord, if good old Dad could see her now.

Her gaze traced the prominent veins running down the inside of Dylan's forearm to where his large, square hand rested so intimately on her. A small distressed sound escaped her. She fought the urge to rudely awaken him. Given his current position, it could do her no good, and she'd rather be spared the embarrassment of him knowing how close he'd gotten to her in the night. She didn't want to waken him only to find herself gazing into his midnight-dark eyes from mere inches away. Her position was compromised enough as it was without having to endure either his cold disdain or—even worse—his hot regard.

Damn him. He was captor and savior. The man lived too much on the edge with no middle ground. There was no place to be comfortable with him.

As well there shouldn't be! her offended sensibilities chorused. He'd kidnapped her at gunpoint . . . and saved her life . . . and tied her up again. Another groan escaped her. Lord, she wished he would move his hand and stop breathing in her ear.

A hushed, whispery sound drew her attention to the window again. The mattress was sliding down the window, pushing the chair before it, and allowing sunlight into the room.

That's what had awakened her, she realized. The room had been pitch-dark when Dylan had turned off the lights to sleep. Now she could see, and what she saw gave her a glimmer of hope—her first. Having him so close on her side of the bed might be the stroke of luck she needed. If he'd had her pulled over to his side, she never would have seen where he'd hidden the phone, let alone been able to reach it.

Using the slack he'd left in her bindings, she worked her right hand down to the phone cord snaking under the bed. The phone made a lot of rattling noise as she pulled it out onto the carpet, and she was sure he was going to wake up at any second. As nerve-racking as the thought was, she kept pulling the cord. He would either wake up or he wouldn't, she told herself. If he did, he would be angry. But he'd been angry with her before and she'd survived. According to him, that was the entire raison d'être for her abduction—her survival. He didn't want Austin to kill her.

Well, neither did she. At least they had that much in common.

The phone came into view on the floor. She scooted closer to the edge of the bed, stopping only when he groaned in her ear. Her heart missed a beat in the ensuing surge of panic, then started back up at an accelerated rate.

Holding her breath and stretching her fingers to their limits, she managed to knock the receiver off its cradle. It thudded to the floor. She slanted Dylan a look out of the corner of her eye and then, ever so carefully, leaned over the side of the bed and punched in Henry's office phone number.

It would have been quicker and easier to dial 911, but a lawyer in crisis wanted nothing so much as another lawyer, and despite his deplorable methods, Johanna believed Dylan. Austin having police connections that could infiltrate and retrieve information even from so lonely an outpost as Laramie, Wyoming, was no more unbelievable than what she'd been reading in the newspaper. Influence peddling, extortion, assassination. Nothing seemed beyond her ex-employer—except Henry Wayland's integrity. Henry was a man a woman could trust, unlike Dylan Jones, who could only be trusted as far as it suited him.

She finished punching in the phone number and managed to get a grip on the receiver. Privacy for her conversation was out of the question, and given the silence in the motel room, she didn't know which would be most likely to lull her captor in continued sleep—a whisper or a quiet, normal tone of voice.

She went for quiet and normal, mostly because she didn't think she could get past Henry's secretary with a mysterious-sounding whisper. Mrs. Hunt had yet to accept the change in hierarchy brought about by Johanna's addition to the firm.

"Henry, please," she said when the office answered. "This is Johanna. It's urgent."

"One moment," Mrs. Hunt responded after a slight, condemning hesitation.

Johanna closed her eyes and prayed for the old bat to put her through and for Henry to take the call. Henry was also having a little trouble adjusting to the new equal partner in his firm. She knew he preferred his mornings quiet and his clients in the afternoon. She knew he preferred tea at 10:00 A.M. rather than crisis. She knew he preferred her to be on time and the secretaries to be early, which of course Mrs. Hunt always was.

"You picked a hell of a morning to be late," he said, coming on the line, and she knew he expected a damn good explanation, despite the fact that she owned half their partnership. "You wouldn't believe what's been going on here all—"

"I'm in Laramie, Henry," she interrupted him. "The Colonial Inn Motel. I haven't got much time. There's a man, Dylan Jones, alias Dane Erickson. Check him out, inside out, upside down, and backward. I want to know everything about—"

"A man?" Henry repeated, his tone quickly changing. "You're in a Laramie, Wyoming, motel room with a man?" He sounded incredulous, as well he would, given his long-standing interest in her total lack of a love life.

"It's not what you're thinking, Henry. I'm tied to the bed."

What Henry said to that was unlike any combination of words she'd ever heard out of her staid partner's mouth, even during their college years. It was more like what she was used to hearing out of Dylan Jones's mouth.

"I don't believe it." Henry swore again, and she could practically see the pained expression come over his face and the way he rubbed the bridge of his nose under his glasses. "You meet some strange man with an alias, for crying out loud, and end up getting left alone in a motel room in the middle of God knows where, tied to the bed, and I've got bullet holes in the walls!"

"Bullet holes? What do you mean bullet holes?"

"I mean bullet holes, Jo-han-na. Like somebody went through here with an Uzi. The office was broken into last night. Trashed. There's nothing left of your files and damn little left of mine."

"My God." She'd never dreamed Austin would go that far. That he would be so desperate.

"It's got to be the James case," Henry said. "And if that bastard thinks he can scare us off with—"

"Henry," she interrupted.

"—strong-arm tactics and—"

"Henry."

"—intimidation, he's going to find out he's messed with the wrong lawyer. I'll put him six feet under so fast, it'll make his head swim."

"It's not the James case, Henry," she said in exasperation, then froze as the man on top of her moved in his sleep.

Dylan murmured something unintelligible and shifted the position of his free hand, sweeping it up from the juncture of her thighs to her right breast. Johanna held her breath until it hurt, then let it out all at once, trying to ignore his natural response to fondle what now filled his palm. The man was too crude for words. She wanted to hit him and didn't dare. She had to get away from him, far away.

"What do you mean it's not the James case?" Henry normally didn't like being corrected, and his verbal attitude told her this morning was no different in that respect.

"It's not James. It's Austin Bridgeman," she explained, whispering into the phone. "You must have read the papers this weekend. Morrow Warner, the company splashed all over yesterday's front page with a senator in tow, is his, Bridgeman's, and I'm the attorney who put it together."

"Bridgeman?" Henry repeated. "The man you worked for in Chicago? You're going to have to speak up, Johanna."

"I can't."

Henry swore again, then forcibly calmed himself. "*Fine*. Have it your way. Tell me where you are and I'll call the police, get somebody in there to untie you." He sounded like he didn't believe what depths he was sinking to in the name of friendship.

"Don't call the police, Henry."

"Dammit, Johanna, haven't you been listening to me? I can't come up there myself this morning! My God. This is exactly what happens when you take up with some stranger because of some wild, hormonal deviation—"

"Henry."

"—of lust arousing magnitude—"

"*Henry*. I am fully clothed and have been all night, so stop thinking what you're thinking."

"You should have called me, Johanna."

"I did. I am. Right now." Lord, she thought, had he always been this sanctimonious? "Henry, listen to me. I am not alone. The man who kidnapped me is—"

"Kidnapped?" Henry interrupted, his voice going cold.

"Yes. Get these names: Dylan Jones and Dane Erickson. He was Austin's number-one bodyguard up until a couple of days ago. He says he kidnapped me to protect me from Austin."

"And why in the hell did he do that? What's his involvement with you?" Henry's holier-than-thou attitude had taken a nosedive into confusion.

Johanna looked down at the man cradling her close to his body and didn't know what to say. What was their involvement with each other? Stolen glances and a promise of protection that had taken four months to deliver? What had he seen in her that had brought him out of the night like an avenging angel to put himself between her and danger?

Her gaze slipped to the bindings around her wrist. He had compromised himself with his treatment of her. He'd broken laws with every step he'd taken, doing more to ensure her safety and her anger than her undying gratitude.

"I'm not sure," she said to Henry. "He says Austin wants me dead, and from what I saw of Austin and his cohorts last night, it's not a difficult thing to believe."

The phone went silent on both ends for a long, frozen moment, during which Johanna imagined how her office looked riddled with bullet holes, an image she was sure was uppermost in Henry's mind. Then he spoke.

"You say this man is a professional bodyguard?"

"Yes."

"Maybe you better stick with him, until he can get you in to the police."

Johanna hated to admit that there wasn't any "maybe" about it. She looked down at the man lying so close to her. What he'd done was awful, criminal, but it was also a miracle. She had never seen anybody get the better of Austin Bridgeman—until last night when a wild man had shoved her into the corner of an elevator, then dragged her down the street virtually under Austin's nose without getting caught.

"He doesn't trust the police," she said to Henry.

"His kind never do."

"He says Austin is too well connected."

"He's probably right, in which case we've been on this line too long. You better get out of there. Call me at the club when you've changed locations, and I'll send the police for you. When they come, tell your bodyguard to stay out of the way. Or better yet, tell him to give himself up. I'm not going to take my partner's kidnapping lightly, whether he saved your life or not. Dammit, Johanna. Bullet holes in the walls!"

The line went dead in her ear, and Johanna hung up on her end. Henry had a plan. Better than hers, she admitted.

So why wasn't she buying it?

Dylan woke to a world of throbbing, pounding pain and an insistent, feminine voice calling his name from close quarters.

"Mr. Jones. Dylan. Wake up. Come on, wake up. We have to leave."

She was shaking him and moving him, and he didn't want to be shaken and moved. He wanted to be left alone where he'd been, hazily asleep in the dreamworld with the soft weight of her breast in his palm and his groin pressed up against her thigh. She'd felt so good, until she'd started shaking him and moving him.

"Mr. Jones."

She shifted again, and he realized her hand was flat on his belly, pushing against him. That was nice. Real nice. Arousal began thrumming through his body, enticing him with the promise of more pleasure. He sighed and, with a slow, natural move, eased himself up and settled into the warm heat of her palm.

Johanna stiffened, mortified. Her hand was trapped, and Dylan Jones was so far out of line she would have screamed if he hadn't chosen that moment to pull her further beneath him and angle his mouth over hers. He moved with the slow surety and precision of a man whose body was fine-tuned to withstand the physical demands of his job. He moved like a man who was finally waking up.

There was no gainsaying the weight of him pressing her into the bed, or the strength of his arm moving her to a more comfortable position against him, or the mastery of the mouth conquering hers. She tried to beat at him, but instead found her hand brushing against the pillow as he tunneled his fingers through her hair, dragging their bound wrists together toward the top of the bed.

Damn him. She'd thought about what his kisses would be like so many times it was pitiful, and now that he'd finally done it, everything was wrong, horribly wrong—the place, the circumstances, the timing. Not even in her wildest daydreams had she imagined anything like what he'd put her through so far, and then for him to have the damn nerve to wake up and kiss her.

"Mr. Jones!" she gasped when he lifted his head for a moment. His only response was a groan and a resettling of his mouth on hers into an even deeper kiss.

With astonishing ease he slid his hand down over her hip and thigh to bend her knee and bring her closer. She struggled and squirmed beneath him, then immediately realized her mistake as his breathing grew ragged. Her leg was tied to his, and squirming only made their contact more intimate.

She didn't bother calling his name again when the opportunity arose. She could barely breathe through the anger he was building inside her. But breathe she did, the one name guaranteed to put the fear of God in him.

"*Austin,*" she said, and his hands stilled.

Slowly he lifted his head, his eyes still closed.

"Austin," she repeated. "Austin Bridgeman."

Dark eyes opened to the barest slit, his gaze fixed on her mouth, unwavering. He looked like he wanted to eat her for breakfast, lunch, and dinner, then start all over again. She felt the heat of his excitement running through his body. His skin was warm, nearly hot to the touch. His breath was uneven, his body pressed against hers in the most carnal of ways.

Her anger, so righteous only seconds before, was having an unbelievably difficult time not getting scorched to cinders by his slow, intense perusal.

Beneath lowered lashes, his gaze drifted to her silk-covered breasts. He looked confused, and aroused, and in pain. Johanna tensed, her pulse racing. She had no idea which of his feelings was going to win out. The moment stretched in unbearable anticipation before he lifted his eyes to meet hers.

"What about Austin?" he asked, his voice gravelly with sleep.

"I—I made a phone call. Henry thinks his line might have been tapped."

"Phone call," he said bluntly. His gaze dropped to the floor and the phone sitting next to the bed. "Damn."

"My office was broken into last night. They tore through all of our files and put a lot of bullet holes in the walls."

"Damn," he repeated softly.

"I think . . . I think we should get out of here as soon as possible."

"You told Henry where you were?" he asked.

She nodded.

"Did you tell him who you were with?"

She nodded again, more slowly.

He held her gaze for another moment, then his eyes traced a still slightly confused, but heated trail back to her breasts. He stared at her for a long time, gathering himself together.

"Damn," he said quietly.

EIGHT

Dylan carefully checked the motel parking lot before lowering himself next to a rusting black pickup. The truck was parked close to the curb at the end of the lot, its front end hidden in a group of evergreen bushes. The windshield was completely busted out, and it was missing a tire in the back, but it had what he was looking for—license plates. In minutes, he'd switched out the front plate with one from the gray sedan and moved to the back of the truck to do the same. He'd left Johanna inside the motel room tied to the bed.

After he'd gotten his bearings, he'd had enough sense to be embarrassed. He had been all over her. She hadn't been pressing herself against him out of desire. She'd been tied to him, her wrist bound to his. She couldn't have gotten away from him if she'd tried. He didn't know what in the hell he'd been thinking to wake up horny and take advantage of her—though he hadn't taken nearly far enough advantage of her to do himself any good.

He swore under his breath. He shouldn't have left her tied to the bed.

The last screw came out of the license plate, and he made the final switch. By now, he knew, the Boulder police would be well on their way to piecing together the gray sedan and his Mustang. They'd have him checked out in Illinois and either would or would not come across his FBI employment, depending on how much the FBI wanted them to know. Johanna's law partner would be throwing a few more scraps of information at the Colorado law enforcers, and it had to be assumed that Austin would get his hands on all the information. So the best Dylan could do was get a new set of plates for the car and resign himself to the fact that he wouldn't be welcome in Chicago for a while and that he better get the hell out of Laramie.

He walked back to the sedan and attached his new Wyoming license plates. He was covering his tracks as methodically as possible. The switch had taken him less than five minutes. He added the five glorious minutes they'd wasted in bed and the few minutes she'd taken to wake him after the phone call, and he figured at worst he had an hour and a half lead on Austin. He was still winning. Last night he'd only been ahead of Austin by a couple of minutes.

Johanna heard Dylan come in and was torn between venting her fury and ignoring him completely. She'd done her part. She'd shown good faith. She'd sewn him up and told him about the phone call, and he'd left her tied to the bed. On top of everything else, she was going to bring him up on assault, and emotional cruelty, and indecent exposure. If she had her way—and up until last night she'd been damned used to having her way—he'd be fighting his way through lawsuits from a jail cell for the rest of his life.

She turned her head away when he started for the bed, but when he touched her, she lashed out.

"Don't touch me."

Her voice was colder than ice and actually gave him pause.

"I'm cutting you loose," he said after a moment, reaching for her bindings again.

"Then do it without touching me."

He stopped once more with the knife blade inches from the tape. "I'm sorry." With a quick upward slice of the blade, he had her free from the bed. He closed the knife against his thigh and slipped it into his pocket before reaching to undo the belt tied around her wrists.

"Sorry?" She turned on him with barely controlled fury. "Sorry? For what exactly are you sorry, Mr. Jones? For abducting me in the middle of night and dragging me, unwillingly, across state lines? For accosting me with a deadly weapon? For that disgusting display you put on in the shower? For—"

"Disgusting display?" he interrupted, his hands stilling in the act of untying her. A small grin tweaked the corner of his mouth. "You're the one who looked, *Miss Lane*. All I did was take a shower."

Color blossomed and spread across her face. He watched her for a moment longer, then finished untying her. She jerked her hands away and called him a bastard under her breath.

He didn't disagree. "I won't apologize for saving your life, no matter what I did." He hesitated for a moment, and when he spoke again, his voice was quieter. "But I am sorry I left you tied up when I went outside, and I'm sorry . . . well, I'm damn sorry about what happened."

He didn't need to explain any further. Her blush deepened to a hotter shade of pink. Ignoring what he'd said, she brushed by him with her head held high. Once in the bathroom, she closed the door with a solid slam and locked it with a rebellious snap of the lock. Dylan Jones could go to hell. She needed her privacy.

Her head dropped to the back of the door, and she closed her eyes. She needed more than her privacy. He had done the unforgivable. He had made her blatantly aware of the sexual energy simmering between them like a pot about to boil over.

Beneath his too-tough exterior, he had a quiet, intense yearning for her that she'd never fully appreciated until he'd awakened in her arms. He'd acted on instinct—pure, and simple, and passionate. She wasn't the type who usually inspired unrehearsed passion. But she'd sensed his desire months ago in his ever-watchful gaze and rare smiles, and a part of her had responded. Now—he'd kissed her, with sensuality and a carnal tenderness she wouldn't soon forget.

He'd also walked away from her, which was the only decent thing he could have done under the circumstances. A disbelieving sigh escaped her, and she shook her head. In less than twenty-four hours she'd changed her opinion of him from a wild, crazed gunman to a decent, passionate man. Next she'd be bestowing sainthood, all because he'd kissed her and she'd felt something beyond the anger she'd held on to so dearly.

An insistent knock on the door startled her out of her reverie. She lifted her head.

"We have to leave. Now." His voice came through the locked door.

She wasn't ready to face him, but he was right. She rubbed a hand over her eyes. Lord, she hated it when he was right.

After hours of driving, the barrenness of Wyoming was beginning to take on a certain appeal. Herds of antelope grazed in the rolling hills, their tawny coloring blending in with the heat-dried grass. Johanna watched eagles ride the wind in an empty, summer sky. She noticed the isolated ranches dotted miles apart across the landscape, and she thought about the women who lived on them.

"I couldn't do it," she said, half to herself, her gaze lingering for a moment on a particularly run-down homestead.

Dylan glanced over and saw where she was looking. The ranch house faded back into the landscape as the miles disappeared under their wheels.

"You could do anything," he said.

"Not that," she said, giving him a surprised glance. For the last fourteen hours he'd dragged her around pretty much at will, making her doubt if she could do anything for herself. She couldn't imagine what made him think otherwise.

She sighed and ran her hands back through her hair, pushing it off her face. She didn't understand him. Of course, she didn't need to understand him. At the next stop she would call Henry at the club, and her life would be her own again—unless Austin got a hold of her first.

Damn, what a mess.

"Are you hungry?" she asked, putting out the effort to be gracious. "I think there's something left from breakfast . . . if you can call what we ate 'breakfast.' " Her graciousness slipped a little at the end, but given the food, she didn't blame herself.

She picked up the fast-food bag between them and dug through the contents. He made a request if she did find anything, and she murmured a reply. She'd had to give up her anger, she told herself. She was stuck with him for a while yet, and anger only wore away at their nerves. At this point neither of them could afford to have their nerves worn away. She felt like warmed-over death, and he was starting to look like it.

She found what he'd requested and delicately

picked up the cold french fry with her fingertips. "You'll eat anything."

"No, I won't," he said, popping the fry in his mouth. "I won't eat stuffed zucchini."

"Stuffed zucchini, mmm." The thought made her mouth water. "Crab and Monterey Jack cheese, seasoned bread crumbs, a fresh salad on the side with mandarin oranges." She picked up another french fry and gave it a dubious look. "I wish you hadn't mentioned it."

"Yeah," he agreed. "You make it almost sound good."

He shifted in his seat, and she gave him a surreptitious look. Lines of strain were etched into the angular contours of his face. A sheen of sweat dampened his brow. She wanted to tell him to pull over so she could check his bandage, but something in his face told her she wouldn't get far with that line. He was on a mission, and they were on the run. Life-threatening infections and wounds had to get in line and wait their turn. Still, she was concerned. More so than was smart.

"Who cut you?" she asked.

He slanted her a wary look. "A Chicago man," he finally said. "We worked together."

"You mean one of Austin's other bodyguards?"

He nodded.

"Why?" she asked.

"We had a difference of opinion."

"Over what?"

He took his eyes off the road for another moment to look at her. "Is this Twenty Questions, counselor?"

She shrugged and looked back out the window, evading his probing gaze. "You're going to need a good lawyer before this is over. I was just doing a little background work."

He snorted. "When this is over, all I'm going to need is a priest."

Johanna didn't know where in the hell her offer had come from. She really had no intention of becoming his attorney. The idea was ludicrous. But she knew his mention of a priest wasn't as flippant as it sounded, and she was surprised at how awful that made her feel.

"Maybe not, if you have a good lawyer," she found herself saying.

From somewhere he found the strength to grin at her. "Who's saving who here?"

"I'm just offering to help you, that's all. It's no big deal."

"Right." His grin broadened and turned wry.

"It's the least I can do," she said, piqued by his casual refusal of her offer.

"No," he said. His grin faded and his expression grew serious. "The least you can do is stay put when I tell you to stay put and run like hell when I ask you to walk away."

She knew what he meant—for her to run if Austin caught up with them, and leave him to face the enemy alone. The awfulness inside her heart welled up and threatened to spill over into tears of frustration. Damn him for making her feel. Damn him for kissing her. Even damn him for saving her life. Whatever had drawn them together that night in Austin's office was supposed to have disappeared, vanished into a past best forgotten. And it would have if she'd never seen him again. He was a bodyguard and she was an attorney, and she didn't need a rocket scientist to tell her the two wouldn't mix.

She didn't believe his FBI story for a minute. If he was FBI, he wouldn't be out here on his own, fighting the biggest scandal to hit the nation in three months all by himself. There would be help, somebody somewhere he could count on besides her.

Dammit.

They drove in silence for a few minutes, until her frustration got the better of her.

"Well," she started in, her tone none too conciliatory, her concern well concealed in anger. "Did you kill him? Are we talking murder?"

Dylan kept his eyes glued to the road and breathed with the pain—in and out, deep and slow. His chest was throbbing. He wanted to ignore her question. He wanted it to slip away unnoticed.

She was looking at him hard, though, burning holes in him with her hazel eyes. He changed his position in the seat again, trying in vain to get comfortable.

"We can probably prove self-defense," she continued in her damn lawyer's voice. "Your body is a mess."

If she thought she was making him feel better, she needed to think again.

"It *was* self-defense," he said curtly.

"Then you did kill him."

His jaw tightened. He hated her a little for making him admit to that. What did she think? That he *liked* killing people? That there wasn't anything more to him than what she'd seen? A kidnapping, car-stealing ex-bodyguard with no place to go but down?

Maybe she was right.

The possibility made him distinctly uncomfortable. How long had it been since he'd heard from the good guys? Two months? Three? It had been before his last contact had been found floating in Lake Michigan. He knew that much.

He also knew he hadn't been on stable ground since his partner, Charlie Holter, had decided to get out of the federal-cops-and-robbers business. Charlie had retired and gone to Seattle. He'd told Dylan to get out too. They could set up a fishing boat together, he'd said, rent it out to high-paying customers, and spend their days angling for salmon out in the ocean. They could have the good life, and didn't they deserve it? They had both put their lives on the line for Uncle Sam, God, and the unwashed masses too many times to count. It was payback time.

Charlie had been right. Dylan should have gotten out. Payback time had come, and he was probably going to end up paying Austin with his life. What a bitch.

"Did I know him? The man you killed?" she asked out of the blue.

"I don't think so," he said, tight-lipped, hoping she would let the subject drop.

"What was his name?"

Dylan silently groaned. Now what in the hell did she want to know that for?

"It will come out in the investigation," she continued. "You might as well tell me."

He tightened his hold on the steering wheel.

"I'm not telling you another damn thing," he muttered, shooting her a narrowed glance. "So if you're smart, you'll stop asking."

He held her gaze for a moment longer in silent warning. She was trespassing, and he wanted to make it damn clear to her that he didn't like being treaded on.

"It's my job to ask—"

He cut her off with a succinctly spoken curse and jerked the steering wheel to the right, simultaneously pulling off the road and slamming on the brakes. A cloud of yellow dust billowed up behind the sedan and was blown forward by the wind, encasing the car.

Johanna's heart lodged in her throat.

"Lady," he began, turning on her with a grim expression tightening his face.

"Don't call me lady," she shot back, edging as close to the rigged passenger door as she dared.

"Okay, *Miss Lane*." His tone was snide, his attitude one of pure belligerence.

"And don't call me Miss Lane. You know my name." She didn't need to see the flash of anger in his eyes to know she was pushing him past the safety zone.

Dylan knew her name, all right. He'd sighed it in

his sleep and awakened with it on his tongue. It had been an invocation to salvation. He'd engraved it on his heart and mind across a thousand miles of prairie. *Johanna.*

"I don't need your help, *Miss Lane*," he said, throwing the car back in gear.

Her hand reached out to stop him. "You're lying, Dylan. From here on out you probably need my help more than I need yours, and you know it."

She had used his name. Her tone was quiet, intense, and her words were disturbingly valid.

Dylan swore under his breath and checked the rearview mirror before pulling back onto the highway. Damn her for being right, even if she was only half-right. She shouldn't have been able to see him so clearly. Dylan Jones was buried deep. His survival depended on the murkiness of his life, the shifting qualities of his values. He didn't like her knowing he needed her, even if she didn't understand how deep his need went—even if she didn't realize just how much of her he wanted.

NINE

Johanna woke up to quiet darkness and an ache all across her shoulders. The air around her was cool, but she was warm. It took a minute of vague disorientation before she realized she was curled up in the front seat of the sedan, covered with Dylan's long coat.

Closing her eyes again, she let out a tired sigh and moved her head. Her muscles rebelled. A low moan escaped her, echoing in the stillness of the car and making her forget her aches and pains.

It was so quiet, too quiet. Where was he?

As if she'd asked the question aloud, he spoke to her.

"That's a good girl. Come on. Wake up, Miss Lane. It's suppertime."

His voice was soft and gravelly, and reassuring. In her sleep-dazed state, it seemed the perfect sound to wake up to, an invitation to warmth and intimacy.

She instinctively turned her head to find him. He was hunkered down in the open doorway on the driver's side of the car, his face at her eye level. The collar of his shirt was flipped up in a haphazard fashion, making him look years younger than he had when he'd kidnapped her. It also made him look in need of a woman's straightening touch—a touch she quickly realized she didn't dare provide.

A wave of sadness came with that realization. Slowly she roused herself to a sitting position, yawning in spite of trying not to, and feeling guilt along with her emptiness. She was the one who had fallen asleep, who had been given the luxury of rest. Yet he was the one who was hurt. He needed something, someone, but it was ridiculous to think for even an instant that it could be her.

"I've already filled the car with gas," he continued, standing up with a stiff, pained movement. "I figured as long as we had to stop, we might as well get a hot meal."

She agreed with a nod, not trusting her voice enough to use it. They had stopped. They were at a new location. It was time for her to leave him.

Fifteen minutes later the waitress in the Elk Café settled two heaping plates of chicken-fried steak, mashed potatoes with cream gravy, green beans, and biscuits with honey down on their table. Johanna inhaled the savory steam rising from the food and sent up a prayer of thanks. They had eaten drive-through hamburgers again for lunch, and she didn't think she could have faced the same for dinner. She'd never felt so junked out in her life.

"Where are we?" she asked, shrugging out of his coat and handing it over to him in what she hoped was a perfectly casual gesture. She'd seen him shiver on the walk inside. The underlying paleness of his skin made her doubt he was capable of warming up by himself, but she had to try.

"Pace, Montana," he said, accepting the coat and putting it on. "Thanks."

"Thank you," she said, lowering her gaze to take a sip of coffee. She knew the coat hadn't been around her when she'd fallen asleep. To Dylan, she'd thought, the coat was not an article of clothing so much as it was a slipcover for a shotgun, whether he was wearing both coat and shotgun on his body or had them bundled next to the driver's-side door. She was relieved to see him wearing the coat for its intended purpose. She was also relieved on another score.

For the first time since he'd kidnapped her—or saved her life, she conceded—he didn't have the shotgun with him. He was still armed, though. Before they'd left the car, he had pulled the tails of his shirt out of his pants and stuck a handgun in his waistband. Whether it made sense or not, the handgun didn't seem as menacing. She didn't hold a personal grudge against it the way she did with the shotgun, which he'd used to threaten her.

"And where are we going?" she asked, digging into the hot food and making idle conversation. She wouldn't be going any farther with him. He'd made it clear that he didn't want her help, and the Elk Café in Pace, Montana, seemed as good a place as any to end their relationship—if what they had could be termed a relationship. Regardless, Henry was waiting for her call.

"Seattle," he said.

She made a noncommittal reply and continued eating, all the while trying to disregard the image of him caring for her by tucking his coat around her sleeping form. It was an act of gentleness, something she had trouble attributing to him. Violence came more naturally to mind.

So did passion.

Her cheeks colored. She hadn't forgotten how it had felt to be kissed by him that morning. He had been warm and had tasted good, very good, despite her anger. She had liked the sureness of his tongue in her mouth, the heated tenderness of his lips and teeth grazing her skin. Enjoying his kiss had been part of what had made her so angry.

She cleared her throat in private embarrassment, not daring to look at him until she'd banished her illicit thoughts. When she was sure she had everything under control, she lifted her gaze and asked, "What's in Seattle?"

"A friend, Charlie Holter, my ex-partner. I'll leave you with him, and hopefully Austin will follow me."

She watched him for a moment, then lowered her gaze to her plate, an action to match the sinking feeling she had inside. She didn't want to think about leaving him alone to face Austin. The situation was too much her fault. The danger he was in was too much her responsibility.

Damn him. He'd had no business putting himself in the middle of her problems. She wasn't at all sure why he had gotten involved, and she wasn't at all sure she dared to find out, which left her feeling guilty and confused, and something else she didn't want to name.

"Where will you go?" she asked, pushing her food around on her plate, her appetite having suddenly disappeared. She needed to know what he was going to do, where he was going to be. She couldn't just walk away from him and pretend his problems were no longer hers.

"I'll head for Mexico." He cut off a piece of his chicken-fried steak and swirled it through his gravy. "Dane Erickson has a lot of connections down there."

"Drug connections," she said, not bothering to phrase the two words as a question. She knew what he was—a two-bit hood who had parlayed street toughness and a finely honed sense of criminality into an uptown career as a bodyguard. She would be wise not to forget that. Unfortunately wisdom seemed to be deserting her in direct proportion with the amount of time she spent with him.

Dylan paused with the piece of steak halfway to his mouth, hesitating as her words sank in. With a quick movement he finished off the bite. He'd be damned if he let her ruin his appetite.

Apparently, though, she wasn't working under the same set of ground rules.

"Excuse me," she said, pushing away from the table.

He'd grabbed her wrist before she had a chance to get her hand off the table.

"Where are you going?" he demanded quietly.

Her eyes flashed in irritation, and she answered him very slowly. "To the bathroom, if you don't mind."

He did mind. She hadn't been out of his sight or control in nearly twenty-four hours, and that's the way he liked things. She may have felt safe in the backwater wilderness of Pace, Montana, but he did not.

He kept his fingers firmly wrapped around her wrist. His gaze held hers, daring her to contradict his unspoken order to sit back down. Then, beneath his hand, he felt the tension leave her arm.

"Let go of me . . . please."

There was that word again, so softly spoken, undermining his instincts and playing on his guilt. He knew he had to release her, but before he did, he tightened his grip for an instant and let his thumb slide across the tender skin of her inner wrist. The gesture was more of a caress than a threat, more of a caress than he'd meant to give. He pulled his hand back, disgusted with his inability to control his reaction to her.

Without a word, she left him, and he sank back into his chair. He had one more night to get through before he left her in Charlie's care. After that, it would just be him against Austin.

He looked out the window fronting the restaurant, glad to be situated farther back in the recesses of the dining room. Bright parking lot lights from the adjacent gas station lit up the outside as if it were broad daylight. The people in the front row of booths were sitting ducks by his way of thinking.

He checked his watch, automatically timing her. He didn't want to give her enough rope to hang herself, or give anybody else a chance to get to her. Until they made it to Seattle, she was his responsibility. Until they made it to Seattle, she was still his.

The Elk Café was part of a larger conglomerate including a gas station, convenience store, and gift shop. Johanna found the telephone next to the bathrooms near the back of the gift shop. Guilt assailed her again as she punched the buttons to place a collect call to the private club where she and Henry were members.

Guilt was ridiculous, she told herself. Nonetheless she also had to keep telling herself it was for Dylan's own good too. She could help him more by using the law against Austin than she could ever help him on the run. Maybe she could even save him.

Save him from Austin just long enough to throw him in jail for your own reasons. That's what she'd threatened him with. That's what she'd told Henry she was going to do. Now she knew she wouldn't hound him into a jail cell. He'd been through enough on her account. More than enough.

Her finger paused above the last numeral in the club's phone number. Her mouth tightened. Damn him for messing up her code of ethics. She knew the difference between right and wrong. Or rather, she used to know the difference. Dylan Jones had made her whole system of values look mighty gray.

She didn't know what to do—but she knew what she would have done yesterday or any other day before he'd come back into her life. She punched in the last number and gave her name to the answering computer. The call was accepted by the first person who picked up the phone. The Boulder Club didn't as a rule accept collect calls from its members, but Johanna knew Henry would have taken care of all the small details. What she didn't expect was to be speaking to a police detective rather than her partner.

"Miss Lane, I'm Detective Campbell. We've been waiting for your call. Are you okay?"

"I'm fine," she said, trying to hide her unease. "Is Henry Wayland there?"

"Yes. Are you still with Dane Erickson? Is he armed?"

"May I speak with Henry, please." Dylan's lack of faith in the police must have rubbed off on her, because she felt surprisingly uncomfortable talking to a detective—especially to one asking questions about him.

There was a moment's silence.

"Miss Lane," Detective Campbell began again, "we've been worried about you. I'd like you to give me your location so we can send someone to pick you up."

"I would like to speak with Henry, please."

A disgusted sigh was followed by the sound of muffled voices.

"Johanna." Henry came on the line, blunt and to the point. "Where are you?"

"What's going on, Henry?" she asked. It had sounded like a lot of people were huddled around the phone at the Boulder Club.

"What's going on?" Henry repeated, his voice rising. "What's going on is that you've been kidnapped by a *certifiable criminal*. Dane Erickson has a rap sheet a *mile long*. Now I want you to quit analyzing the situation and just tell us where you are so we can *get you the hell out of there*."

A woman walked into the alcove concealing the bathrooms and the telephone, and Johanna turned her face to the wall to keep the conversation private.

"Relax, Henry. I'm safe."

"No, you're not. You are definitely not safe. Your Dylan Jones, alias Dane Erickson, Daniel Erickson, and Marty Barnes, has been up on charges from car theft, to check bouncing, to three counts of assault. He's never gone as far as kidnapping before, but it fits. He's a dangerous man, Johanna."

"I knew he was a car thief."

"Are you listening to me?"

"Yes."

"He's been implicated in some very major drug dealings."

"In Mexico, I know."

"The police would *love* to pick this guy up, but they're more concerned about your safety. I must have been deranged this morning to suggest that you stay with him."

A man came out of the men's room, and she turned her back the other way, keeping her eyes downcast and her voice low.

"I didn't have a choice this morning, Henry. I was tied to him."

"Right." Henry sounded relieved that the decision had truly been out of his hands. "But you're free now, thank God, and you need to tell us where you are. Don't worry about Dane Erickson. He won't be able to hurt you once the police have you. They are professionals, Johanna. They know how to handle men like him."

Men like him. She dragged her hand back through her hair. Johanna didn't even know where men like him came from, let alone how to handle them. She'd never met anyone more compelling or so quietly, seriously confident of his abilities, and she'd known both those things the very first time he'd walked into Austin's office. She also knew she didn't like the idea of turning him over to the police.

"Henry, I—"

A movement at the opening of the alcove caught her eye. She glanced up, and her heart stopped for an instant. When it started up again, it was beating too fast. Her mouth went dry. Dylan leaned back against the wall and slipped his hands into his front jeans pockets, watching her with a brooding gaze. His coat was draped over one arm, helping him hide the gun in his waistband.

"It's a miracle he hasn't done any jail time," Henry continued as if she hadn't spoken. "All I can think is that he's got a damn good lawyer."

Dylan shifted his position slightly, and Johanna stiffened, bracing herself. Henry said something else she didn't catch. Her concentration was all on Dylan and what he might do next. The possibilities seemed endless and none too pleasant.

With effort, she held his gaze, until his lazy, dangerous perusal shifted to a more questioning, less condemning countenance. Then she had to look away. He was giving her infinitely more grace than she deserved. It was his life she was juggling, her net he'd gotten caught in, and she who had been caught red-handed betraying him.

She wanted to say she was sorry, but the words wouldn't come. For a moment she was gratified she had at least a semblance of honor left, however fleeting. But a fleeting sense of honor wasn't enough to save him. He'd turned her world upside down, and consequences would be paid. One word and she would be free of him. It was the only sensible thing to do, but she couldn't remember when being sensible had ever seemed so wrong.

Her gaze moved back to his face. He was tired, weary. The strain of his life showed in the pinched lines at the corners of his eyes and in the unconscious movement of his hand upward to support a bruised rib. He breathed slowly, watching her, waiting for her to answer his silent question.

She was in emotional quicksand and sinking fast.

She needed to leave him, but she couldn't. He wouldn't survive without her. Nothing could be simpler, or more compelling: He had saved her life; she had to try to save his.

"You're right, Henry," she said, lowering her gaze and speaking softly into the telephone. "He does have a damn good lawyer."

"Jo—"

She hung up the receiver and faced Dylan with what she hoped wasn't a look of pure, unadulterated guilt or total surrender. "I guess we better get going. I'm not sure if they traced the call or not."

He took his time with an answer, letting his gaze drop partway down her body and come back up before he nodded and turned to leave.

The look made her nervous. It implied a willingness to accept a concession she was sure she hadn't intended to make. Yet she wasn't willing to change her decision.

Halfway across the parking lot, his steps slowed. She thought he was hurting and looked up at him in concern. He didn't return her look, but surprised her by taking her arm and gently pulling her to a stop.

"There's something I need to know." He seemed strangely ill at ease, even shy in the way he failed to meet her eyes with his usual domineering attitude.

"I didn't tell them where we were or where we were going. I promise," she said.

"Why not?" he asked, tilting his head to face her, and she realized that was the question he wanted answered. "You had the chance. I wasn't going to stop you."

She stared up at him for a long moment, then lowered her lashes. A pale flush of color came into her cheeks.

It was apparently all the answer he needed. He released her arm and touched her once, lightly, on the shoulder, guiding her toward the car.

Johanna was mortified. She wasn't sure what he'd read into her reaction, but she was sure embarrassment was an appropriate response on her part. She should have given him her reasons in a straightforward, professional manner. Instead she'd equivocated and given him a free field to come up with his own answers.

"I believe you're with the FBI," she said belatedly, trying to salvage her reputation as a woman with above-average intelligence.

"Good."

"Henry checked you out. He didn't come up with the FBI, but he said you've never done any jail time. I drew my own conclusion."

"Correctly," he added, reaching for the passenger door on the gray sedan.

Too late Johanna realized what he was doing. She inhaled sharply and whirled around, throwing herself against him and almost knocking him down. It had been her intention but he was too quick, too steady on his feet. His arms came around her, holding her tight, and she buried her face against his chest, holding her breath for the instant it would take for a blast of sound and pressure to end their lives.

The blast never came. His heart continued to beat a strong and solid counterpoint to her ragged breath. The warmth of his body continued to envelope her like a protective shield.

"Damn," he muttered, his embrace tightening. "Dammit. I'm sorry, Johanna."

The door had not exploded. He'd been lying to her all along. She didn't know whether to sob in relief or shout at him. In the end she did neither. She pulled herself together with as much dignity as she could muster, called him a bastard in a very ladylike manner under her breath, and got in the car.

He closed the door for her, and she couldn't help but flinch. For twenty-four hours she'd been expecting the damn thing to blow up at any minute, and it hadn't even been armed.

"I'm sorry," he said again after he'd gotten in and closed his own door behind him. "I guess I could have told you this morning."

"You could have," she agreed in an affronted tone of voice, an amazing feat considering how badly she was shaking inside.

"I did it to keep you from getting hurt."

"So you say about everything." Her pulse was still racing, and she was afraid she might burst into tears at any moment.

They sat in the dark, in total silence, until he finally spoke.

"I was hurt pretty bad last night. I knew I didn't

have much time to get you out, and I didn't think a wrestling match in the car would do either of us any good."

The first tear came, unbidden and unwelcome, but Johanna didn't know if it was for herself or for him.

"I've been pretty rough on you," he admitted. "I wish . . . well, I wish it could have been different."

So did she. Another tear tracked silently down her cheek to join the other. She wished everything could have been different—because months ago, when Austin had first introduced her to his newest employee, she had thought Dane Erickson was someone very special. Now she knew she'd been right.

TEN

Out of the corner of his eye, Dylan saw the shine of wetness on her cheeks. Wary, he turned his head to see her more fully. He'd always known there were certain levels of the female psyche he was unfamiliar with, but the depth of his ignorance hit him anew.

What was she crying about? he wondered. They hadn't blown up. She now believed he wasn't a complete reprobate. So much of the worst was over for her. Wasn't it?

Her soft sob and quick inhalation told him otherwise. He had an uneasy feeling the crying business was only beginning. When she sniffled, he knew it.

He let out a heavy sigh and glanced around the parking lot. He knew how to fight with her, and God knows he'd dreamed enough about making love with her, but tears were beyond his coping abilities.

Maybe she'd just figured out that she'd made a

big mistake by not giving him away to the police. He glanced over at her again.

No, he decided. She was too smart not to realize she'd done the best thing for herself as well as for him.

"The Bureau gave Dane Erickson a record," he said, turning halfway toward her and addressing what he thought might be part of the problem. He'd heard enough of her phone conversation to know Henry Wayland hadn't wasted any time in checking Dane Erickson's "references," as it were. He'd also surmised that the FBI had chosen to retain his cover—typical of the type of support he'd been getting for the last few months. "Your lawyer friend probably found out about it."

"He did." She discreetly wiped at her cheek with the heel of her palm, but he saw the gesture and it pulled at him in places he hadn't known he'd possessed.

"The drug thing was also set up by the FBI," he reassured her. "On the whole I'm a pretty law-abiding citizen."

Johanna slanted him a disbelieving look through her tears.

"You always impressed me as a woman with good instincts," he continued. "I guess I just want you to know that you can trust what they've told you about me."

His audacity amazed her.

"What in the world makes you think that might be to your advantage?" she asked, her disbelief rising along with her eyebrows.

He shrugged and reached under the steering column. "You're here, aren't you?"

The wires he twisted in his fingers sparked the engine to life, thankfully overriding the necessity for her to answer. Because of course was right. Again.

With dismay, she dropped her head back on the seat and closed her eyes. Her actions had spoken for themselves. They didn't need her big mouth confirming everything he was thinking.

Dylan eased the gray sedan out of the parking lot, carefully watching the traffic. Maybe he'd stated his case too bluntly. He'd obviously made her angry— again—a particular talent of his, he realized. But she'd stopped crying, and for that he was truly grateful. He was too far down the line to be discovering personal weaknesses like Johanna Lane's tears.

Miles later he pulled off the highway and followed a dirt track back into the mountains, heading for what a billboard had promised would be a Rustic Resort with Family Cabins, a Restaurant Lodge, Horseback Riding, and World-Class Trout Fishing with Professional Guides.

The sky had never looked darker or the stars brighter than they did under a crescent moon in the Rockies. Dylan wasn't exactly sure where they were— other than someplace in northwestern Montana—but he took that as a good sign. If he didn't know where they were, neither did Austin.

"I thought we were going to Seattle, to your friend's," Johanna said, shortly after he made the turn off the highway.

"We are."

"We're getting a little out of the way here, then, aren't we?" she asked, echoing his own thoughts.

"That's the general idea."

Another mile of silence passed before she spoke again. "How long have you lived in Chicago?"

"Most of my life. I was born there." If she wanted to talk, that was fine with him. It helped keep his mind off his pain and his exhaustion. Pace, Montana, was supposed to have been their stopping place for the night, but she'd blown that possibility with her phone call.

Hell, he didn't blame her. He would have done the same thing.

"As a city boy, doesn't all this bother you?" she asked, and the nervousness in her voice made him turn and look at her.

"All what?" he asked, confused. He could think of three or four different things about their current situation that bothered the hell out of him—and none of them had anything to do with being born in Chicago, Illinois. He didn't have a clue as to what was troubling her, but his list started with her name.

She was bundled up in his coat, her back straight, her bottom perched on the edge of the seat, as far on her side of the car as she could get. That bothered him plenty, because he wanted her close to him. The more he thought about it, the closer he wanted her—close enough for their skin to slide over each other's, for their breath to mingle, and the taste of her to become a reality on his tongue.

Great. Now he was really bothered, *hot* and bothered.

"All these trees, the forest, the dark, the stars," she said, missing his problem by a light-year or two. "We haven't passed a town in over an hour. It actually looks like there could be . . . well, *bears* out there, lurking around."

"You're too old to be afraid of the dark, counselor," he said wryly. "And I've never heard of anybody being afraid of the stars."

"That still leaves about eight million trees and Lord knows how many bears." She didn't sound at all convinced of his reasoning or her safety.

He gave her a thoughtful look before he spoke. "You can't possibly be afraid of the trees."

She grinned sheepishly at him, the last thing he'd expected. "Okay," she admitted. "It's the bears. There are bears out there, aren't there?"

He was quiet for a moment, then he turned to hide his grin and swore, one succinct word. A second's worth of laughter escaped him, and he swore again. "I can't believe it."

"What?"

"Bears?" he asked, incredulous, turning back to her. "Bridgeman is after us. Half the cops in Colorado are after us, and by now, if we're lucky and they're doing their job, the Feds are after us. And you're worried about bears?"

"A bear is a dangerous animal," she said in her own defense.

"So is Bridgeman," he countered, not able to give

up his smile completely. "Don't worry, Miss Lane. I didn't drag you across three states and the Rocky Mountains to let a bear get you."

"Thank you," she said softly, seriously.

He slanted her a quick glance. She was still bundled up in her corner of the car, but her posture had relaxed. His gut tightened, and he bit back a curse. She had no business trusting him like that.

He went back to watching the road before he got himself hurt by falling in love. Then her sigh drew his attention back to her face, to the elegant curves of her cheek and brow, to the satiny texture of her skin and the marring smudges of weariness he'd put beneath her eyes, and he knew it was too late.

The owner of the Rustic Resort was just putting up the "Closed" sign and turning out the lights when Dylan pulled up. Dylan's first thoughts were that "lodge" was an overstatement of the size and grandness of the main building, a bit of marketing misinformation exceeded only by the use of the term "resort." "Rustic," however, was right on the mark.

A line of cabins curved along either side of the "lodge," following a bend in the river, their outlines barely discernible against a backdrop of dark sky and forest. A barn and corrals were on the other side of the dirt road, their structures easier to see in a broad, flat pasture that gathered the sparse moonlight and used it to silver fence posts and shingles.

"Maybe you better come in with me," he said,

shifting the car gear into park. "A woman is harder to turn down in the middle of the night than a guy who looks like he just lost a bar fight."

"Okay." She slid across the seat toward him, catching her mistake halfway there. He stopped her when she started to reverse direction.

"Come on. It's okay." He took her hand and pulled her after him as he got out of the car. He closed the door behind her, but he didn't let go of her hand. "Try to look tired."

"I am tired." Johanna fell into step beside him, wondering about their hands. The small intimacy felt both awkward and pleasant. His palm was warm and dry, comforting in the cool, dark night.

"When we get inside, I'm going to tell the manager you're my wife. It would be nice if you'd back me up."

"If it'll get me a bed and a bath, I'll tell him I married you twice."

"Once will be enough." He tightened his hold on her hand and his thumb stroked down the side of hers.

As a gesture, it wasn't much. But it was enough to remind her of exactly what she'd done by hanging up on Henry. It was enough to remind her that she hadn't left Dylan when she could have—when she should have.

He'd killed a man to save her life. She didn't have a doubt about that. He'd arrived at her doorstep still bleeding from the fight. The knowledge frightened her the way knowledge of any act of violence was frightening, but it also left her with a deep sense of a debt owed. The men Austin had brought with him had destroyed an expensive suite of offices with an automatic weapon. She doubted less and less that they would have done the same to her. Dylan knew those men, knew what they were capable of doing, yet he'd pitted himself against them and Austin, risking his life to keep her alive.

She wanted to give him something in return, but she didn't know what or how, not within the limits of gratitude she was unsuccessfully trying to define. Her support in a lie designed to get them a place to stay for the remainder of the night wasn't much. Holding his hand was little more.

Inside the lodge office, the owner—Gus Orbison, he told them right off the bat—was happy to open up and rent out another cabin for the night. The older man's eagerness to help them had more to do with financial gain and Dylan's surprising transformation to a congenial good old boy, Johanna knew, than any amount of yawning and wifeliness on her part.

"Now," Gus said, "I have one super deluxe cabin that I rent out for seventy dollars a night. That includes your firewood, a bathtub instead of a shower, and a scenic view window. The whole place is going super deluxe, one cabin at a time, as the boys and I get around to it."

"Sounds like a bargain, Gus." Dylan gave the old man a broad grin and reached into his pocket for his money. "Anything exciting ever happen around here?"

"Nothing ever goes on around here 'cept a card game in the back. If you're not too good, you're welcome to join me and the boys." He looked up at Dylan from under bushy gray eyebrows and chuckled. "Got me a couple of real smart wranglers this summer, college boys from Spokane. They're good with the horses, but they don't know a damn thing about poker."

"I'm too tired to fleece anybody tonight, but maybe I can sit in tomorrow," Dylan said, thumbing off a few bills.

"Tonight's your only chance," the old man warned, accepting the cash. "The fishing guides get back from upriver tomorrow, and they're a wily bunch. Damn wily."

Dylan laughed. "Maybe I just better stick to fishing then."

"Well, you came to the right place for fishing. Half a mile upriver starts the best stretch of Gold Medal water in the state." Gus pulled a key off the board behind him. "Number nine is the last cabin on the south end." He handed Dylan the key with one hand and pointed with the other. "You can't miss it."

"Thanks," Dylan said. "What time does your restaurant open in the morning?"

"Well, we've got a fisherman's special starting at four A.M., which is a pot of coffee and a couple boxes of doughnuts I'll put out yet tonight. We serve a full breakfast buffet at six-thirty when the cook gets here."

"Great. See you then." Dylan placed his hand on Johanna's elbow and guided her back out the door.

"I'm not getting up at six-thirty for breakfast," she told him on the front porch.

"Okay," he agreed—or so she thought. "We can wait until seven."

"Noon."

"Seven-thirty."

"Let me sleep until nine and I'll split the cost of the cabin."

"Better be careful, counselor," he said, sending her a wry grin. "You're going to have a hard time laying claim to my Mustang if word gets out you've reimbursed your abductor for kidnapping expenses."

"I'll take my chances with the courts," she said around another yawn.

At the sedan, he opened the door for her, but she balked.

"I can't get back in that car," she said. "I may never be able to get back in that car."

Dylan knew she was only half teasing, because he felt the same way. He was damn tired, and damn tired of being crammed into the gray sedan.

"Okay. Let's walk." He slid partway in and reached under the steering column to disconnect the ignition wires. Then he grabbed the duffel bag out of the back. If anyone was going to spot a stolen car at the Rustic Resort, the two hundred feet between the office and cabin number nine wasn't going to make any difference.

And if Austin found them in the backwoods of Montana, Dylan would rather Johanna stayed put with a super deluxe cabin around her than making a run for a tin can of a car. He'd have to check out the surrounding area, see what kind of protection and cover was available for himself and the bad guys. He'd slept with the shotgun last night. He would check all of his weapons tonight.

"You're thinking awfully hard," she said, walking beside him. "About Austin?"

He nodded. "He's got an advantage over us. While we're sleeping he's still got enough men to keep the search moving." A pain lanced through his knife wound, making him wince. "Damn."

"Are you okay?" She touched his shoulder, a gesture of caring he hadn't expected.

"Yeah," he said, his voice rougher than he'd meant it to be. He tried to rest the duffel bag against his leg as he walked, to relieve some of the weight pulling across the front of his chest. Looking up ahead, he saw they were about halfway to the cabin.

In the next moment she'd moved closer and wrapped her hand around the carry strap of the duffel bag. "Let me help."

They finished the distance in silence, her shoulder brushing against his biceps on every other step. The night wrapped around them in pine-scented darkness, the quiet broken only by the sound of their breathing. Dylan tensed, trying not to think about her nearness. He was an easy mark for her softness tonight, and for all his aches and pains he wasn't worn-out nearly enough not to want it.

His gaze slipped to the woman beside him. He'd put her through hell, and there was no denying his actions had made their mark on her. Her hair was a mess, finger-combed and tousled. She didn't have a speck of makeup on, and her clothes looked like they'd been slept in more than once. What he wanted from her, though, what he had always seen in her, went beyond makeup, expensive clothes, and the stylish cut of her hair.

He shouldn't have been surprised last night when she'd stood up to him. She'd stood up to Austin under many trying circumstances, always keeping one foot firmly planted in the law. He'd watched Austin bluster and blow and demand the impossible from her, and he'd watched her give it to him time and again. When Austin had come to the realization that she was a woman above and beyond her legal skills, he'd also watched her come to the decision that because of her employer's sexual interest, it was time to resign.

She had strength, integrity . . . and great legs. God, he was a fool.

Unlike the other cabins, number nine opened onto the river to take advantage of the scenic view out the single window. Dylan smiled for a second in wry satisfaction as they walked around the cabin.

"What?" she asked, her awareness of the subtle shift in his expression surprising him.

"This place," he said.

She looked at the small building. "What about this place?"

"It's built like a fortress. Gus and the boys just slapped up new logs around the old cabin. The walls must be two feet thick." He pointed to the riverbank sloping away from them to the water. "We have the high ground, what there is of it, and they don't have any room to maneuver. If they want us, they'll have to come in the front, and I don't think Gus is going to take kindly to anybody who shoots out his scenic window. He had a rifle behind the counter in the office. An old boy like that isn't afraid to use it."

"I didn't see a rifle," she said, helping him carry the duffel bag up the porch steps. They set the bag down while Dylan inserted the key into the lock.

"You weren't looking for one," he said. "I hope you can come out of this still not looking for guns."

"Yes," she agreed, her voice soft.

He glanced down at her, but she looked away.

"It must be hard," she said, "living the way you do, always on your guard, always expecting somebody to hurt you."

"The idea is to hurt them first," he said, opening the door and stepping aside.

"Yes." Her voice was even softer, as if she understood all too well how he operated and, worse, felt sorry for him.

It galled the living hell out of him.

She turned the light on in the cabin. He followed her with the bag and closed the door none too gently behind them. She turned, startled, at the noise. Her gaze immediately went to his shirt, and a gasp escaped her.

"You're bleeding again." She stepped toward him.

"Leave it," he growled, grabbing her hand when

she reached for him. Her surprised gaze collided with his, but he didn't relent. "Just leave it."

He didn't want her pity, and he sure as hell didn't want her ministering to him like he was some damn invalid. What he wanted, what he wanted so very badly . . . was her kiss.

ELEVEN

"But you're injured," Johanna said, standing very still in front of him.

"It's not going to kill me."

The bones in her wrist were small and delicate. Dylan could feel her pulse beating in the palm of his hand, racing.

"And that's where you draw your line, isn't it?"

"Yes. That's where I draw my line."

God, she was beautiful. With his free hand, he traced the cool, sweet curve of her jaw.

"It's getting you hurt," Johanna said, trembling from his touch, from compassion, and from anger that for whatever reason, he didn't take better care with his life. She tried to pull her captured wrist free, but he held tight.

"The only hurt I'm worried about," he said, his voice growing husky, his fingers curving around to cup her chin, "is if it's going to hurt me more to kiss you . . . or to let you go."

Endless seconds slipped away. His eyes grew darker as he tilted her head back, telling her full well what he had decided, what they'd both already known. She had time to resist him, and when she didn't, he slowly settled his mouth over hers.

Dylan did nothing else for a long time, nothing except inhale her fragrance and lose himself in the chaste kiss, nothing except hold her chin to keep her from moving away. The action took no effort at all; he did it with his fingertips.

Her lips were soft and lush, her skin smelled uniquely feminine, everywhere like a woman. Each breath he took of her followed an endless spiral of desire deep down to his inner core.

Gently, so gently, he shifted the angle of his mouth over hers, parting his lips as he did. With the slightest movement, she leaned into him. It wasn't much, but it was more encouragement than he had expected, and much more than he needed.

A groan he'd had no intention of releasing echoed between them as he opened his mouth and claimed her as his. He had killed a man to save her life, to know the warmth and beauty of her would live on after he was gone. She was his one good deed.

So he took the kiss as far as he could, pulling her body close to his, where her touch could ease away his pain. He stroked the silky insides of her mouth with his tongue and dreamed of her other secret places. He threaded his fingers through her long honey-blond hair and plundered her mouth, taking his forbidden taste—a taste she more than allowed with every moment she stayed within his embrace.

Every sigh, every caress of her tongue on his lips was like adding tinder to a bonfire. The pleasure of her response burned through him like a fiery white light. He wanted her, he could have her, now.

Johanna was sinking fast, unsure of her course, yet so sure of wanting him to hold her forever. The kiss was madness, and she was trapped in the middle of the maelstrom by the intensity of the man urging her to relinquish even more of herself to him. In spite of his weakened state, his body was all lean strength and corded muscle, powerfully male, and it brought out her most feminine needs, needs she was used to ignoring. But Dylan Jones, lately of Bridgeman, Inc. and improbably of the FBI, a kidnapper of proven expertise and frightening success, made ignoring her needs impossible.

"Johanna." He whispered her name, his mouth sliding across her cheek to her ear, his hands slipping under her T-shirt to cup her breasts. Kneading her, he gently bit her jaw, and her neck, and the top of her shoulder through her silk shirt.

No one had ever moved her more deeply, or so quickly. He triggered emotions so far down inside her, she'd never felt them in all their richness, neither all the pleasure nor all the pain. He brought her both: the searing physical pleasure of his body moving with hers, the heat of his mouth, of his life's breath warming her skin; and the emotional pain of knowing she desperately wanted something she couldn't have.

"Don't," she whispered, drawing him to her rather than pushing him away. She buried her face against his shoulder and felt the fierce pounding of his heart. Her eyes closed on a ragged breath. "You were wrong. It hurts more when you kiss me."

Dylan wasn't buying it. He drew in an uneven breath, tightening his arm around her. She was holding him as if she might die if she let him go, and she'd kissed him with the same kind of passion. Women were different from men, and the differences were their allure—the softness, the mystery, the way they gave, and what they took. Sometimes they understood things differently than men, and sometimes they didn't understand things at all. He didn't think Johanna understood where they were in their situation. Forces stronger than his willpower and her objections compelled him to explain in every way possible.

"It'll be worse if I stop," he promised her, sliding his hand down over her hip and pressing his groin against her. "Much worse, I swear."

Before she could react or deny him, he lifted his head and captured her mouth once more, his fingers and thumb wrapped around her jaw to hold her for his kiss. Every dream he'd ever had of her, he took the opportunity to realize. He laved the tender inner skin of her lips with his tongue and mimed the act of love in her mouth, and he fell deeper and deeper under her spell, wanting and needing more of her—until she started to give.

Surrender came in sweet, rolling waves: the feel of her hand in his hair, the fullness of her breasts pressing against his chest, the slight lift of her hips beckoning him closer, welcoming him.

It was simultaneously too much and not nearly enough. He caught his breath and swore silently, pulling her harder against him to increase the pleasure building in his loins. God forbid if she should change her mind. He was already past the point of no return.

Johanna gasped as he rubbed himself against her and kissed her shamelessly. She was under siege, her body and her emotions. His arm was like a steel band around her waist, commanding and relentless, yet his hands and his mouth touched and teased her with an aching tenderness.

She'd had her chance to say no, hours ago in Pace, Montana. The look he'd given her when she'd hung up on Henry had been fair warning, and still she'd come with him . . . because she'd wanted this, to know him once in love. Gratitude was a minor part of her motivation. Lust even less so. Her need for him, to be a part of him, went beyond her power to reason. There was no reason to want him as badly as she did.

She did want him, though, with all her heart. She wanted to soothe him and cherish him. She wanted to kiss him with all the tenderness he was showering on her. She wanted to give him pleasure in being alive.

Under the pressure of his fingers, the snap on her jeans gave way.

"Yes," she murmured, covering his mouth with hot kisses.

With no hesitation and little finesse, Dylan took her to the bed, lying down with her amid the pillows. He cushioned her head with his palm as he continued to kiss her, driving his tongue deep in long, sure strokes. The victory of finally having her beneath him was exquisite. The pleasure ricocheted down his body like summer lightning, touching him everywhere.

"Lift your hips," he whispered between kisses, then pulled her jeans down her legs when she did. He sat up to finish undressing her and found her reaching for his chest again.

"You're still hurt." Her fingers touched his shirt, close to where he'd been knifed.

"Yeah, I know," he said, pulling her shoes off and dropping them over the side of the bed. "But let's just do one thing at a time. Okay?" He looked at her from under his lashes and flashed her a grin.

The underlying sensuality in that rare smile of his was her undoing. It brought the mischief back to his face, the implicitly sexual mischief he'd promised her more than once when their eyes had met across Austin's office. His smile had been the tease, the come-on she'd waited for during Austin's long-winded tirades. Dylan's smile had been the lifeline she'd looked for when Austin had started stalking her like bedroom prey instead of simply admiring her as a boardroom advantage.

"Okay," she agreed, pushing herself up and slipping out of her jeans. She dropped them over the side of the bed to join her shoes. A smile of her own graced her mouth, and she began unbuttoning his shirt. "And the first thing we're going to do is take care of you."

She opened his shirt, and her fingers were on the corner of his bandage before he caught her hand.

"You're working a little high, counselor," he said, sliding her hand lower, down over his chest. With his other hand, he unbuckled his belt and opened his pants.

"You need to be taken care of," she insisted.

"You're right." He kissed her, moving his mouth over hers as he drew her hand ever lower. Slowly he pushed her back on the bed and slipped her hand beneath his waistband. "So take care of me, Johanna."

His message was clear, his method of delivery provocative, and his request undeniable. He filled her hand with his heat and desire, making her want to touch him and hold him, to stroke him until his pleasure ran over into her.

"Dylan . . ." The breath went out of her on a shuddering sigh as he responded with a groan.

"Yes," he urged her, keeping to the rhythm she set.

He stripped off her underwear and began his own sensual exploration of her body. Smoothing his hand over the sleek, creamy skin of her curves from breast to hip, he remembered everything he'd missed about not having a woman, and realized everything he'd missed by not having her.

But she was his tonight.

"Johanna." He sighed her name and threaded his fingers through the soft curls at the apex of her thighs. Every atom of his being told him to take her, to imprint himself on her and take more than she knew she had to give. She was his salvation—not from Austin, nothing could save him from Austin—but from dying alone for no reason other than that he had stayed in the game too long and gotten caught.

Johanna Lane would remember him, and he wanted those memories to be passionately alive, to last. He wanted to give her the very best of himself and as much of the truth of Dylan Jones as he had left.

He took a hold of her wrist when to let her continue her sweet torture would only leave her unsatisfied and him wishing he'd been able to wait.

"Dylan?" she asked, her voice questioning and breathless.

"I want to make love inside you," he told her, smoothing his thumb across her brow and pressing his lips to her forehead. "And I want you to be naked when I do it."

The color that washed into her cheeks brought another smile to his face. He rolled onto his back to shuck off his jeans, then took the rest of his own clothes off before he came back and helped her slip out of her T-shirt and bra.

"You are so beautiful," he murmured, running his hand down the line of her throat to her breast. He followed the path with his mouth, then lifted his head to meet her eyes. "I used to spend a lot of time wondering what you looked like without your clothes." His glance strayed down her body. "I know a lot of people do that, it's human nature—but with you, it was different. I'd watch the way your hips moved when you walked and be damn impressed that any physical action could be so smooth, that such a relatively small movement could have such a profound effect on me. I should have been immune, but I wasn't. And counselor"—his hand swept down over her hip to her thigh—"I didn't have it even half-right."

"Dylan," she whispered, and he pulled her beneath him, laying his body along the length of hers.

"You were important to me from the first day we met, and I can't tell you how many times I wished I'd kissed you that night."

"I'm not sure we would have stopped at a kiss," she confessed, looking up at him with surprising shyness, considering that they were almost as physically close as two people could get.

A slow, easy smile curved his mouth. "I can guarantee we wouldn't have stopped at a kiss."

His hand glided across the top of her leg and up her inner thigh until he touched the soft core of her femininity. He stroked her there and watched a lambent light darken her eyes and take the shyness away. His smile faded.

"Don't forget me, Johanna," he said, his voice hushed as he pushed into her, making the contact he had craved. Her gasp of pleasure was all the invitation he needed to take her higher.

Don't forget me . . . don't forget me. His entreaty tore at Johanna's heart while his body made her forget everything except that he was with her now, for this moment of time.

She gave him everything. Where he touched her, she opened herself and gave him back warmth and welcome. She touched him in turn, and with her fingertips and the palms of her hands told him he was beautiful. She whispered words of love she should have kept to herself, yet she retracted nothing. She let him have her ego and her pride, because he had given her life. The man of her dreams was more than she'd ever imagined him to be, more courageous, more tempting, and more in need of her love.

When she felt him quicken inside her, she wrapped her legs around his waist and held him. The tension he created inside her increased in waves of intensity until he came to the point where his surging slowed in speed and built in power and grace, filling her deeper, pushing her farther.

"Dylan . . . Dylan." She clung to him, her back arching in the purest physical release.

Dylan covered her mouth with his, sealing them together and taking the sounds of her surrender inside himself and adding them to his own.

She was his. In triumph and ecstasy, she was his.

He held her long past the time when he could have let her go. She was warm and sweet in his arms, her body trembling, her lips moving in a gentle caress across his shoulder and down the curve of his biceps.

He'd weakened himself immeasurably by loving

her. His state of relaxation was so complete as to be dangerous, yet he couldn't keep a smile from flirting with his mouth. He felt so good. Turning his head, he kissed the soft skin of her neck and buried his face in the crook of her shoulder.

Moments later, his breathing grew soft and even in the quietness of sleep.

When Dylan awoke to sunlight several hours later, he was alone.

TWELVE

Panic grabbed at his gut. She was gone.

Dylan swung his legs over the side of the bed and grunted at the pain that shot through his chest. A bloodstained towel fell into his lap. He stared at it a moment, confused, then he realized she must have pressed it to his wound while he was asleep—before she'd run off to her damn my-partner-Henry-Wayland, or the police, or to who knew the hell where.

He swore furiously. He'd been suckered by the oldest trick in the book—*pun intended*. She had been sweet and willing, and he'd taken the bait, hook, line, and sinker, and lost himself in the love he'd felt.

Damn her.

To think she'd been lying to him last night hurt more than he would have admitted to anyone, himself included. He clenched his hand into a fist.

He couldn't have been that wrong about what had happened between them. He had trusted her, and he hadn't thought he'd ever trust anyone again. His paranoia on that score had saved his life more than once. Extreme caution was an ingrained habit. Watching his back was the cardinal rule. Those kind of convictions weren't overcome by a beautiful face and a great pair of legs, even if the great legs were wrapped around him. It took something more.

No, he had not been wrong about Johanna Lane. She wouldn't have left him . . . but she could have been taken.

The thought no sooner formed than he discarded it. Austin would not have left him alive under any circumstances.

So where the hell was she?

Lifting his head, he took a breath and tried to slow the racing of his heart. Early-morning light, vague and hazy, spilled across the middle of the cabin, showing him most of what he'd missed the previous night: the mellow pine paneling, the moss-rock fireplace and blue hearth rug, the cowboy lamp on the dresser, the autumn-leaf pattern in the curtains. He looked out at the scenery framed by the window and saw heavy mist and fog rising off the river.

The smell of coffee slowly brought his head around. A plate of doughnuts and an insulated coffeepot were sitting on the bedside table. He felt the first edge of fear ease. Gus didn't do room service; the food had to have been Johanna's idea. The duffel bag with his guns and clothes was at his feet, and the shotgun had been leaned against the wall next to the headboard, as if whoever had put it there had had plenty of time to organize things the way they liked, or the way they thought he might like things organized.

Gus definitely wouldn't have touched his gun. Johanna, on the other hand, would have known exactly where he'd expect to find it if he needed it. He started to relax, but not enough that he could do anything except pray she hadn't gone so far he couldn't find her damn quick.

He pushed himself to his feet, stifling a groan. His legs didn't feel too steady. As he reached for his pants the door opened, slamming his adrenal gland into overdrive.

Propelled by instinct, he lunged for the shotgun and swung it around, pumped and ready to fire.

"Hi," she said softly after a heartbeat of terror had passed over her face, leaving her pale and wide-eyed. She stood half inside the doorway. "I was afraid this might happen."

"What?" His finger was on the trigger and his pulse was going a hundred miles an hour in an erratic, breath-stealing rhythm.

"That you might accidentally shoot me if I came back inside. I got to thinking I'd made a mistake by putting the gun where you could get to it. But I knew you'd be safer if it was in reach." She paused and made a helpless gesture with her hand. "I should have knocked, or something, but I didn't want to wake you up if you were still asleep. I stood out there on the porch for five minutes before I decided to take a chance."

"I'm sorry." He slowly set the shotgun down on the bed behind him, trying to prove to both of them that he was in control. "I'm not quite awake."

"You move pretty fast for someone who isn't quite awake," she said, still holding her ground by the door.

"It's called an overload of survival instinct. It's not a very comfortable thing to live with." He ran a hand through his hair and attempted a smile. "It's okay to come in."

She didn't look like she believed him.

"It makes me nervous to have you stand in the doorway like that," he added, trying to coerce her inside where she would be safer.

It occurred to him then that he was buck-naked, and from the way her gaze fell, he could tell it was occurring to her too. Of its own accord, the temperature seemed to rise in the room.

"Better be careful, counselor," he warned her softly. "Like you said, I can move pretty fast for someone who isn't quite awake."

His teasing brought a wry smile to her mouth. She looked up at him with one eyebrow raised.

"I think if it came to that, I could outrun you this morning," she said. "I've had my coffee, and I'm wide-awake."

"Yes, but I've got motivation."

"Me too," she said, closing the door behind her and crossing the room. "I'm motivated to look at your wound this morning."

"What I have in mind is more fun," he assured her, following her with his eyes as she bypassed the bed and headed into the bathroom. She was wearing one of his clean shirts, the tails tucked into her jeans, the collar flipped up. It was big on her, but he liked the way it looked. He liked having her wear his clothes.

"No doubt." She disappeared into the smaller room, and he heard the water start running in the bathtub. "Are you going to come in here, or do I have to come out there and get you?"

He took a bite of doughnut and reached for his pants, grinning widely. She was still with him. He was still winning.

With less trouble than he'd anticipated, he managed to get his pants on and zipped up. He'd been living on adrenaline for too long, and letting go of it last night with her had left him sore and aching, able to feel the tension he'd been nursing into steel knots in his muscles and joints for three days and nights.

"Dylan," she called.

He took another bite of doughnut and poured himself a cup of coffee. He wasn't going in there without coffee.

"Dylan."

He looked over his shoulder and found her leaning against the bathroom door, a no-nonsense expression on her face.

"You shouldn't have bothered to put your pants on," she said. "I'm only going to take them off you again."

A grin eased its way across his mouth. "And I thought this wasn't going to be my lucky day."

It was his smile more than his innuendo that caused Johanna's composure to slip. That sensual smile made promises she knew he could keep if she gave him half a chance. She hadn't tired of kissing him the night before, not nearly. When he'd fallen asleep in her arms, she'd kissed him dozens of times, light feathery kisses on his face, neck, and shoulders, trying to tell him even in his dream state that she cared for him.

And she did care for him, more than was sensible or wise. If it didn't hurt so badly, she might have admitted to loving him. But love, and emotional survival, and Dylan Jones did not mix. It was better to make love with him and tell herself she did it out of compassion and because no one had ever touched her the way he had—not because she loved him.

"You have cuts on your legs," she said. "I want to see them too. So you're going to have to take your pants off."

He started toward her, still grinning. "You're either going to get embarrassed or in trouble."

"I'll take my chances."

"You've been doing a lot of that lately," he said, stopping just in front of her. He reached out and caressed her cheek with the backs of his fingers. "I was worried when I woke up and you were gone."

Scared senseless was more like it, but Dylan wasn't going to admit to that.

"I went for a walk. It's very peaceful outside, and very, very quiet." She grinned. "I don't know where all the animals are, but I didn't see anything. No Bambi. No Thumper. No Smokey."

"If we had time, I could show you."

"I thought you were a city boy, born and bred."

"Yeah, but even city boys like to get out into the woods whenever they can."

"In case you didn't notice, there are no woods in Chicago," she informed him with a knowing tilt of her head.

"My dad lives in Minnesota, the northern part."

"And your mom?" she asked, her face softening in curiosity.

"She lives in Florida now. But when I was growing up, we lived in Chicago."

"Divorce?"

"I always thought 'broken home' was more descriptive of what happens when a man decides to trade in the middle-aged worn-out wife who bore all his children and get himself a younger bed partner. The second Mrs. Jake Jones is only two years older than my oldest sister. Lily has never forgiven my father for that."

"You have a sister?" she asked, her surprise evident.

"Three, and one brother."

"You come from a family of five children?" Her gaze narrowed, as if the question were an accusation she didn't quite believe herself.

"Yes," he said warily, not quite sure why the news was so shocking. "I'm the youngest."

She just looked at him for a minute with an emotion he couldn't define darkening her eyes. Then she turned her back on him and pointed at the toilet. "Sit there."

It was a command, not a request, and he complied while she readied the first-aid supplies she had piled around the sink.

"So where are they? All these sisters and your brother?" she asked, her voice tight.

"Pretty much spread from coast to coast. Lily is still in Chicago, Kevin's in Boston, Brenda's in Florida with Mom, and Erin lives in San Francisco."

She ripped open three sterile bandages and slammed a roll of tape down next to them. "And they let you run around like this? All by yourself? Hurt, and bleeding, and in danger?"

"I'm a big boy, Johanna, and this isn't exactly their line of work." He was relieved to know something more serious wasn't bothering her.

"Somebody should be helping you." She twisted the hot-water tap on and threw a washcloth into the sink.

"You're helping me."

"*I mean somebody else.*" She turned on him, hands on her hips. "I mean somebody who cares for you, like a brother or a sister, or someone who is responsible for you like the damn FBI you keep telling me you work for. Where in the hell are they? Why aren't they helping you? Helping us?"

Now she was getting close to dangerous territory, asking about his rogue status. He had asked himself the same question a hundred times over the last few months, and he'd come up with the same answer all one hundred times.

"I don't think they trust me," he said, keeping his voice nonjudgmental.

"They don't trust you?" She didn't sound like she believed him.

"I don't think so." He laughed a little shakily and shook his head. "They've been cutting me loose for weeks, setting me up for something I've been trying damn hard to stay out of. I don't know what."

"Why wouldn't they trust you?"

"A couple of people were killed, a couple of their people. I'm sure they thought I should have been able to prevent what happened."

Her prolonged silence told him what she was thinking even before she spoke.

"The man from Chicago, the one who cut you, was he one of their people?"

She was using her lawyer's voice on him. He didn't blame her—not too much—but it ticked him off.

"Johnny Shepherd, also known as Johnny the Shark, was no federal agent," he said. "He was a southside pimp before he got promoted to work as a piece of body armor for Austin Bridgeman. Nobody's crying in their beer over losing Johnny Shepherd, least of all the Feds."

"Is he the message you left Austin in Lincoln, Nebraska?"

He wasn't going to answer such an incriminating question, and the look he gave her told her as much.

"Will there be a murder charge?" She rephrased her words to the same effect.

He held her gaze steadily with his own. "I don't think they're going to be able to find anyone to hang it on."

Her face paled, and she turned away from him as his meaning sank in. "Don't say things like that."

"I'm just being realistic," he said, rising to his feet and slowly turning her back around to face him. "The only way I can stay one step ahead of Austin is to face the facts and take them for what they are, good and bad."

"Are there any good facts?" she asked.

"Other than you? Damn few." He slid his hands up her arms and pulled her closer. "Something was going wrong with this case from the very beginning, and I've never been able to figure it out. When that happens, it can only be because somebody with more authority than you doesn't want you figuring it out. They're withholding information. That's what got the other two agents killed, not me."

"So go to somebody with more authority than the person you think is keeping information from you," she said, her voice lifting hopefully.

"The last person I went to is dead," he said bluntly. He didn't want her getting her hopes up for him. He didn't want her losing sight of reality. Lord knows, he was trying damn hard not to lose sight of what lay ahead. He'd lied to her about what he was going to do after he stashed her with Charlie. He wasn't heading to Mexico and hoping Austin followed him. He was going after the bastard, and he had every intention of killing him if he got the chance. It was the only way to protect her. It was the only chance she had of seeing next week, let alone living to a ripe old age. His own chances didn't look nearly as good. He knew exactly how well protected Austin was, and he knew exactly what he'd have to do to get through that protection.

She lowered her head to his chest on a heavy sigh and closed her eyes. "That's a bad sign when your superiors start dying, a very bad sign. There's got to be something we can do."

"You've done your part," he said, brushing his lips across her temple. "And if you'd like"—he lowered his mouth to her ear—"you can do it again."

She looked up at him. "I'm serious."

"So am I, counselor." A suggestive light warmed his eyes and put a half smile on his face.

"Last night wasn't a civic duty. I'm not with the DA's office."

"And making love with you again isn't going to change my chances, but I want to do it anyway . . . very badly." His mouth came down on hers, hot and sweet, and his body eased up against her, rocking gently, reminding her of how good it had been in the night.

Johanna allowed the kiss, because she couldn't resist, but she refused to be dissuaded from the job at hand. Slowly but surely she felt him come to the realization that if nothing else, she was serious about playing doctor.

"I'm not going to win this one, am I?" he asked between shorter kisses.

"Not for about ten more minutes. That's all I'm asking. I'm worried about you. I need to see what kind of damage I did to you, and see if I can do a better job." She stepped away and turned to shut off the bathwater.

"I don't think I can take another suture," he told her. "I was pretty wired the other night, and having you sew me up seemed like a sensible idea. I'm more relaxed now, and it seems like a crazy thing to have made you do."

"I promise, no more sutures. But we need to disinfect and rebandage." She picked up a box of cotton swabs.

"I'll tell you what, counselor." He took hold of her hand and relieved her of the swabs. "You give me those ten minutes alone in here to get cleaned up. Then I'll let you do anything you want with me."

"Do you need help with your pants?"

He glanced down at himself and saw her do the same. When their eyes met, a smile he couldn't help graced his mouth and brought a blush to her face.

"If I get into trouble, I'll let you know. Okay?"

"Okay," she said, backing out of the bathroom, her blush deepening for every degree his smile broadened.

THIRTEEN

Dylan looked down at the woman in his arms and traced the curve of her shoulder with his hand. She was resting her head on his abdomen, her breathing in rhythm with his, the soft, silky strands of her hair trailing over his groin.

He had bathed, then let her rebandage him to her heart's content, an indulgence that had paid off in the healing caresses of her fingers over his body. Making love with her had made his renewal complete.

He breathed deeply, stretching his muscles, and she slid her hand up his chest. God, he could get used to having her with him, to having her kind of tenderness in his life. He was already addicted to the pleasure.

With no more reminder than the trace of his last thought, he felt arousal spread once more through his loins. He slowly pushed himself up and lowered his mouth to hers, rolling her beneath him.

There was no getting enough of her.

Johanna sat on the edge of the bed and finished buttoning the shirt she had borrowed from him. Dylan was asleep behind her, still resting in what had turned into an early-morning nap—or so she thought until his arm came around her waist and brought her back down to his side.

"Impossible," she said, shaking her head at him before she leaned forward and gave him a kiss. "You can't possibly . . ." Her voice faltered as he moved her hand across the top of the sheet and placed it between his thighs.

"Don't underestimate yourself, counselor."

"It's you I've been underestimating," she said, her face suffusing with color.

He laughed softly at her blush. "I know. Me too." A smile that was both cocky and self-deprecating teased his mouth. "It's almost embarrassing, wanting you like this."

"I never meant to embarrass you." She lowered her lashes and lightly stroked him beneath the sheet.

Dylan groaned and tightened his hand on her waist, reacting to the rush of sensation caused by her touch. He closed his eyes and felt her slip away, down his body. Then his breath caught and his heart started pounding. She took him in her mouth, her breath warming him, her tongue tracing paths of dampness and lightning up and down the length of him.

His next groan came from deep in his chest and the one after that from even lower as she slowly and deliberately drove him closer to the edge of bliss. He floated in the sheer, sweet passion of her wantonness, receiving the most intimate gift of her love, until his need to be inside her became a consuming passion all its own.

"Johanna," he said through his teeth. When she didn't respond, he reached down and ran his hands through her hair, lifting her. "Come here."

Her eyes were glazed, her body like liquid fire heating his skin as she came to him. Rolling to the side, he pinned her beneath him and spread her legs with his knee, making room for himself between her thighs.

"I'm going to make you mine," he promised, then buried himself inside her with one deep thrust, sheathing himself in her heat. He captured her cry of surprise with his open mouth and pushed into her again, his body shaking. His rhythm was strong and unrepentantly meant to seduce her beyond the boundaries of given love, his goal nothing less than the same total surrender he felt building inside himself. He'd never before wanted so much from a woman. He'd never before wanted a woman to be his so completely.

With another man Johanna would have fought such a forceful claiming. He asked for nothing, took everything, and gave no quarter—all with an overwhelming intensity. He was Dylan, his actions said, and she was his. He would accept nothing less, he wanted nothing more.

In her heart she had been ready and willing to give him everything, but she hadn't truly known what everything could entail. The man above her had known, and he was teaching her with the driving force of his body what it meant to belong to only one man and no other.

He dominated her with his strength, holding himself above her with his hands clenched into the sheets next to her shoulders. His repeated invasion crossed the border from pleasure to pain and back again.

"Dylan . . . stop," she gasped. She needed time, she needed a breath. She needed control over what was happening.

What he gave her was a kiss—a kiss to steal her heart and soul. The sweet laving of his tongue through her mouth was sensory overload and her final undoing. The different tastes of him mingled into one and spread like a magic elixir through her pores. When he moved his mouth to her breasts, she cried his name.

"Oh, Dylan. Yes. Yes . . ."

He wrapped his fist in her hair, forcing her head up to meet his gaze. "Look at me, Johanna," he ground out, his body straining for completion, sweat slickening his skin. "Look at me and take me."

Take him she did, for she had no choice, neither physically nor emotionally. She wanted him from the depths of her being, a place she'd never known she could share until Dylan Jones had forced his way inside.

His climax came with a mighty groan that echoed in her heart. She clung to him as the shudders of release racked her body, completely his in the final act of dissolution.

"Don't you dare," she whispered long minutes later when he slowly traced the line of her hip with his hand. Her voice was a bare murmur coming from where she lay curled up next to him.

"I couldn't," he assured her, rolling onto his side and lowering his head next to hers. He lay there quietly, breathing in her fragrance and smoothing his palm across her skin. She was so silky and soft. The feel of her was something he would never forget.

"We have to get ready to leave soon," he said after a while. "We still have a lot of ground to cover before we get to Seattle."

"I don't want to move." She eased herself even closer to him. "I may never want to move again."

"I need to call Charlie to set up a meeting place. Let him know when we might get there. I'd like to make the drop as clean and as fast as possible."

She stirred, turning her head just enough to meet his eyes. "By 'the drop' I assume you mean me."

He grinned, and she rolled her eyes at him before lowering her head back down and resuming her serious relaxation.

"I've changed my mind," she said a moment later.

"About sex?" he asked, then added ruefully, "I don't think you changing your mind is going to make much difference. Not for a while anyway."

"No. About Charlie Holter," she said. "I'm not going with him."

His hand stilled on her hip. "Yes, you are."

"No, I'm not," she said clearly, coming up on her elbows. A fall of hair slid over her shoulder. She looked down at him. "You aren't responsible for me, Dylan, and neither do you have any authority over me."

"Yes, I am, and yes, I do, counselor," he said equally as clearly, his expression one that would brook no argument.

"I'm going with you."

"No, you're not."

Her gaze slipped away from his, and she ran her hand over the suddenly tensed muscles in his arm. "What were you and Johnny Shepherd, two Chicago boys, doing in Lincoln, Nebraska?"

Dylan couldn't believe it. He couldn't believe two people could make love the way they'd been doing all morning, and one of those people's minds could still be working like a steel trap—and it wasn't *his* mind he was talking about. His mind still felt like mush, pleasantly so. Damn, she was persistent.

He waged a silent war with himself and her question. The truth was more bizarre than she could have imagined. He hadn't planned on telling her. In truth, he'd half killed himself to make sure she would never know what he and Johnny the Shark had been doing in

Lincoln—but telling her might be the edge he needed to get her to do what needed to be done.

His gaze flicked up to her face. She had to go with Charlie. There could be no compromise.

"We were working on a hit," he said.

"A hit?" Her eyebrows shot up in surprise. "You mean like a contract to kill somebody?"

"Yes."

"My God!" She unconsciously drew herself tighter together, her clasped hands coming up under her chin, her shoulders hunching forward. "You were supposed to kill somebody in Nebraska? I can't believe it."

"No, Johanna," he said. "We weren't supposed to kill anybody in Nebraska." He reached up and slid his hand under her hair, lifting it off her neck and letting it slip back through his fingers. "Johnny and I were sent to kill somebody in Boulder."

He could tell by watching her when the full impact of his words hit home. Shock drained the life from her face, leaving her curiously flat looking. Then, with a strangled sound, she pulled away from him, grabbing for a blanket as she made her escape. He caught her before she was even half off the bed and brought her back into his arms.

"Johanna." She struggled against him, but he held her tight, making his voice soothing. "Johanna, listen to me."

"No."

"Johanna." His tone became more demanding, his grip more firm.

"Why?" she cried. "Why would Austin do such a

thing? That bastard." Her voice softened into tears. "That bastard."

Dylan cradled her next to his chest, understanding all too well both her anger and her fear. He let her cry, knowing the betrayal she was experiencing defied description. Austin had wanted her life. He had wanted her existence annihilated in exchange for an added degree of safety. Dylan knew what it felt like to mean so little, to be expendable. The woman in his arms should never have had to confront such knowledge.

When her tears slowed, she lifted her face to his. Moisture pooled in her eyes, making them appear fluid and rain-streaked.

"What if he'd sent someone else?" she asked. "What if he hadn't sent you? I'd be dead now, wouldn't I?"

"You've been safe from the day I walked into Austin's office and saw you sitting there. I knew then that whatever came down, if you weren't already involved, I'd do my damnedest to keep you out of it."

"Why?" Her brow furrowed in confusion, her eyebrows drawing together.

Dylan didn't know what to say. He hadn't understood his reaction himself. He'd seen her sitting there, looking confident, in control, totally beautiful, and totally out of place. Watching her work that first day, listening to every word she spoke to Austin, he'd known she was flying blind, that however good she was in her capacity as one of Austin's lawyers, she wasn't aware of all of his other dealings.

The way she had kept looking at him, politely interested, possibly intrigued, definitely wary, had been a sure clue to him that she hadn't understood why Austin had taken to hiring bodyguards.

"I thought you were innocent," he said.

"And when you started looking through the papers on Morrow Warner?"

A small smile twitched his mouth. "I thought you were good, maybe too good. You were giving Austin everything he wanted and somehow managing to stay clean. I was impressed . . . and worried."

"Worried?"

"Yes." He nodded. "I wanted an airtight case and you were weaving loopholes."

"Do you have an airtight case?"

His smile faded and his face grew grim. "All I've got is two dead agents who worked with me and a whole lot of evidence nobody seems to want anymore."

"And Johnny Shepherd." She closed her eyes and lowered her head. "My God. What happened that he ended up dead?"

"I'm not sure." He reached up and ran his thumb over her bottom lip. "Are you okay?"

"Yes." Her voice trembled, but he took her at her word. She was stronger than most.

He gave her shoulder one last squeeze, then got up and started putting on his clothes. "Johnny was wired before we even hit the Chicago city limits, and it just got worse. Ten hours in a car with a hyped up copilot flying on cocaine is not my idea of fun. I got a little rude with him, a little crude, making sure he knew who was in charge. He got rude back, told me I better watch out who I was trying to impress, told me he thought he could get a two-for-one deal by taking all of Austin's trash out in one trip."

Dylan buttoned his shirt, then tucked the tails into his jeans before zipping them up. "By the time we got to Lincoln, push was coming to shove, and I knew my cover had been blown. Johnny never would have confronted me unless he thought Austin was behind him, backing him up. The thing that didn't make sense was, if Austin had really wanted me out of the picture, he wouldn't have left it up to Johnny. I got cut a couple of times, but Austin knew I was the best he had. He had to have known Johnny would end up dead, not me."

"Maybe he thought a murder rap would look good on you."

"Maybe," he agreed. "Or maybe Johnny was supposed to put a bullet in the back of my head instead of trying to take me on with a knife. Johnny liked his knife a lot. He'd used it a few times on a couple of his hookers."

The sudden change in her expression brought him up short.

"I'm sorry. I shouldn't have said that."

She shook her head, silently telling him it wasn't his fault. "I should have known what was going on. I knew things were changing, but I didn't realize how deep the changes went. The man who hired me four years ago wouldn't have also hired a man like Johnny

Shepherd." She looked up at Dylan. "He wouldn't have hired you."

Dylan shrugged. "Four years ago Austin Bridgeman didn't need a bodyguard. Some deals went bad. He needed cash, and all of a sudden the rules started changing. I've seen a lot of people get in over their heads that way. Most of them don't come out on top. Austin wanted to make damn sure he did."

When she didn't say anything, he leaned down and brushed his mouth over the top of her head in a brief kiss.

"I'm going to go call Charlie. We'll leave when I get back. Okay?"

"Okay."

He slipped the handgun into the back of his pants and reached for his coat, but when he turned to leave, her voice stopped him.

"Dylan?"

"Yes?" He looked back over his shoulder at her, continuing to pull his coat on.

"Thank you for saving my life."

For a moment he was tempted to tell her he loved her, that he'd had no choice but to do everything in his power, and some things that he hadn't thought himself capable of, to save her life. Not everything had changed, though. He was still taking her to Charlie. He was still going back for Austin. And his chances still didn't look very good.

"You're welcome," he said, and turned toward the door.

❧━━━━━━━━━❧

"Charlie. Dylan here." He stood outside of the lodge, using the pay phone next to the soda-pop machine. He had more privacy there than inside, where late-starting fishermen and a few families were milling around, enjoying the breakfast buffet.

The air was comfortably cool, enough so that his coat wasn't too out of place, though he would have been less conspicuous in a parka or a down vest.

"Dylan! Good to hear from you, boy! Where the hell you been? I've been calling you for three days, must have left half a dozen messages on your machine."

"I'm on a road trip, heading in your direction." It was good to hear Charlie's voice, something familiar. Charlie was older, wiser, and had gotten Dylan out of more scrapes—political and otherwise—than he cared to remember.

"Great! We going fishing, or what?"

"Or what."

There was a lengthy pause, and Charlie's voice changed from lighthearted exuberance to almost sad in its seriousness.

"Are you in trouble?"

"I've got a woman with me, and she's got a contract out on her. I need a place to put her for a few days."

Charlie didn't answer immediately. Dylan hadn't expected him to. The older man had a well-earned reputation for looking before he leaped on all occasions and under all circumstances. It's what had saved Dylan's life twice.

"Can you bring her here?" Charlie finally asked. "Or do you want to meet somewhere?"

"Meet somewhere. In Seattle," Dylan said. Charlie lived north of the city, on the sound. If someone had been able to track them, Dylan would rather they stayed on his trail in and out of Seattle, instead of him leading them to Charlie's.

"Where are you?"

"North of Missoula, Montana. Nine or ten hours from you."

"You'll be here early evening. Let's meet at that bar on First Avenue, the one up from Pike Street. Do you remember the place?" Charlie asked.

"Yes."

"The one where we ate steamed clams and drank so much beer, they had to carry us out of there."

"I remember." Dylan almost smiled. They'd had some wild times together. "We'll be there. I want this to be quick and clean, Charlie. I'll send her in, tell her to go into the ladies' room. I'll stay in the background, you'll see me, and when she comes out, she leaves with you."

Charlie agreed, and Dylan hung up. He felt like a weight had been lifted off his shoulders. He had somebody else on his side now, somebody who could take care of her if he went down.

All he had to do was get to Seattle.

FOURTEEN

"I met Henry at Denver University," Johanna was saying. "We even roomed together for a while."

"Roomed together?" Dylan cast her a skeptical look from his side of the car. They had traveled across Idaho, entering the state of Washington on Interstate 90, and were passing through Spokane.

"We shared an apartment," she explained dryly. "If you ever meet Henry, you'll know it was a relationship based on finances and friendship, and study habits. I function better in the morning, and Henry can barely face the day before noon. We hardly ever saw each other."

"But now you're business partners, Wayland and Lane." Dylan liked listening to her life story, Henry Wayland and all.

He didn't like what lay ahead of them. Leaving her was going to be harder than he'd thought. He was tempted to slow down, take another day, steal another night, just to have her by his side a few extra hours.

"Yes," she said. "Henry didn't leave Colorado after school. I couldn't wait to get back to Chicago, but when I decided to make a change, I remembered how much I had liked it there. We haven't been partners for very long, so we still have some bugs to work out. Like his secretary for one. Mrs. Hunt hates me, and I'm getting tired of it."

"A little female jealousy?"

She flashed him grin. "A lot of female jealousy. She's very . . . uh . . . territorial."

"About Henry?"

"About Henry, and about the filing cabinets, and the law books, and the telephone, and the pencils, and the coffeepot. You name it, she's made it clear that every item in the office has a long and rich history lovingly detailed by her for Henry. She's been there for a long time. Sometimes I think that's why Henry asked me to come on board—to give Mrs. Hunt something to think about besides him so he could have a little breathing space."

If Henry couldn't handle his secretary, Dylan concluded he could pretty well write the man off as competition. He smiled.

"Why doesn't he just get rid of her? Fire her?" he asked. "There's got to be plenty of good legal secretaries around."

"Yes, but probably none who would take his laundry home twice a week and iron his shirts."

Dylan let out a short laugh.

"And bring his lunch every day in little plastic microwavable containers," she continued, "and peel his oranges without the white part."

"You're kidding me," he said, glancing over at her.

She shook her head. "God's truth. I swear. She even makes him scones for his morning tea and spreads the jam all the way to the edge on each one. I've stood there and watched her do it, like she was painting the Sistine Chapel."

"Sounds like Henry hired himself a mother instead of a secretary."

"No. What Henry did was hire his mother to be his secretary."

"Mrs. Hunt is Henry Wayland's mother?" He shot her a disbelieving look.

"She's been married a couple of times since Henry's father passed away." She grinned at him again.

Dylan laughed, then looked back at the road and laughed again.

"Henry sounds like a . . ." His voice trailed off, and he gave her a sheepish smile as he tried to come up with a less offensive word than the one he'd almost used. "He sounds like a wimp."

"Oh, he is," she agreed wholeheartedly. "Except in the courtroom. It's the only place he can handle having conflict in his life, and he loves it there."

"Is he married?"

"Only to his golf clubs. Golf is a religion to Henry."

"Well, everybody needs something," Dylan said

with a sigh, meaning every word. He pointed up ahead at a fast-food restaurant. "Do you want to stop and get something to eat?"

Johanna took one look and groaned. They'd eaten at the same franchise twice the day before, which was twice more than she wished she had. "No, thank you, nothing for me. But you go ahead—though I don't see how you can eat that stuff."

"It's quick and easy." He shrugged and put on his blinker to get off the interstate.

"Food isn't always at its best when it's quick and easy," she said.

"Neither is sex," he murmured half to himself, then slanted her a sly grin. "And between the two, it's no contest. I would much rather have spent the time we had together today making love instead of eating lunch."

Johanna couldn't fault his reasoning. For a moment she thought he was going to say something more, but he didn't, and she didn't push. There was nothing they could say to each other. He didn't want to hear that she wasn't going with Charlie no matter what Austin had done, and she didn't want to hear him say no again.

He pulled into the parking lot of the restaurant, but instead of heading for the drive-up window as he had for their previous meals, he actually parked.

"I thought if we went inside, you might see something you'd like," he said. "They have salads. If nothing else, you should get a milkshake. I don't want you going hungry."

"A salad sounds good," she said, though she had

her doubts about a fast-food salad. Still, Dylan had enough worries without her adding to them. "May I borrow your comb?"

In answer, he leaned over the seat and searched through the duffel bag until he found what she wanted. He handed her the comb, then stuffed the bag back into its hiding place under the seat.

She took a few quick swipes with the comb as he got out and walked around to her side of the car. Running her fingers through her hair in distraction had become almost a compulsive habit in the last two days. She now understood why he had looked so wild when she'd first seen him in the elevator of her apartment building.

She had just finished restoring some order, if not style, to her hair when he opened her door. She started to get out, but an abrupt shift in his gaze warned her that he'd suddenly changed his mind. He turned to block her way, his hand pushing down on her shoulder, guiding her back into the car.

"Sorry, counselor, but we're leaving." His voice was casual, as was his stance, but his eyes told a different story. They met hers with a piercing intensity. "Lean over and open my door, then stay down."

She did as he asked without question. He closed her door solidly behind her and went around the back of the car. When he got in, he immediately reached for the ignition wires.

"There's a man inside the restaurant," he explained. "I don't like the way he looks."

She peeked up over the dash. "What do you mean,

the way he looks?" The sun was hitting the restaurant windows at such an angle as to make seeing anything inside near impossible. She could make out the silhouette of a man, among others, but she certainly couldn't see him well enough to make a judgment call on his motives for being in a fast-food restaurant on the west side of Spokane. She didn't think Dylan could either.

"I can't explain," he said, "but in this game, that feeling is adequate grounds for running like hell. There'll be someplace else to eat down the road a ways."

"Down the road a ways" proved to be over an hour away, a very long, silent hour in which her attempts at conversation had been dismal failures. She was worried about him. Since they'd left Spokane, he'd gotten steadily edgier. Of course, she'd been known to get a little edgy herself when she missed a meal. She was edgy now. Somehow, though, she got the feeling Dylan's problems went deeper than hunger.

"There's another one of your hamburger places up ahead." She pointed out a sign next to the highway and read the directions aloud with a surprising amount of hope in her voice. "Take the next exit, then in a half mile take a left on Stanton Avenue."

"I think we'll pass," he said.

"I know you're hungry," she said, cocking her head in his direction. "So am I, and I really don't mind eating a hamburger and french fries."

"We'll have to stop for gas pretty soon. We'll get something then."

She sat back in her seat, sighing heavily as she remembered the premade, day-old sandwiches of their first night. She wondered if the next service station/convenience store would have better food or worse.

Worse, no doubt, she thought, her mood deteriorating with the knowledge. She was thinking more of him, however, than of her own abused palate. She hated to see his nutrition levels drop even lower than they already were. He needed decent food, and rest, and medical attention.

She bit back a frustrated oath. She would get nowhere appealing to his sense of personal well-being.

"Dylan." She spoke his name quietly yet firmly, determined to get his attention and hold it until she'd said her piece and gotten some answers. "When we were talking about Henry earlier, you said everybody needs something. I need to know what you need. I know we're in danger. I understand the necessity for being careful. But I do not understand why our situation has to preclude taking your basic needs into consideration. We have to stop at a doctor's office. You have to have antibiotics, and I think you should have medicine to ease the pain. We both need to eat, and better than we've been eating. Besides which, quite frankly, I don't think a possible paranoid delusion is enough reason for the two of us to starve to death on the interstate."

That was her piece—and she got damn little in return for it.

She took his silence for a mile or more, waiting impatiently for him to say something. She waited, and waited.

"Dylan," she started again when her patience had grown too thin to bear the weight of his silence.

"This morning," he interrupted her, his patience also obviously at the end, "*you* eased my pain. This morning I thought I had *you*. Now I'm not so sure."

"What is that supposed to mean?" she asked, taken aback. "I'm still here, aren't I?"

"You're here now. But where were you this morning when I woke up?"

She couldn't believe that's what had been bothering him since Spokane. "I was taking a walk. I told you."

"Taking a walk?" He sent her a quick glance. "Or calling Henry again?"

She was stunned into silence.

Dylan saw the hurt on her face, but he didn't take back his accusation. He'd been thinking hard the last hour, and none of his thoughts had been good ones. The man in the fast-food restaurant in Spokane had triggered his warning instincts like a four-alarm fire. He hadn't told her, but besides looking like somebody who was looking for somebody else, the man had seemed familiar. Not in any way Dylan could put his finger on or identify, but he'd felt a definite sense of familiarity. It was a piece of information he was having a hell of a time computing. Kidnapping *was* a federal offense, so it was possible he might have met or worked with someone they'd pulled in on Johanna's case. Or possibly only the man's cautious, searching demeanor had been familiar. Dylan didn't know.

He did know Johanna had called Henry twice before, and that she'd had plenty of time to call her partner that morning. He had inadvertently set a pattern of eating in one particular fast-food place. She could have told Henry where they'd eaten the day before and suggested that they would probably eat in the same place again. The Feds could have staked out a few restaurants between Spokane and Seattle. Austin could have gotten the information and staked out a few places of his own.

So he was paranoid. Who had a better right?

"I didn't make a phone call this morning," she said, anger simmering just beneath the surface of her words, "but you did."

He shot her a stony look. No, he thought. He wasn't that paranoid. Not yet. If Charlie had wanted him dead, he'd had plenty of chances during their five years together.

The last hours into Seattle were the longest of Johanna's life. She thought they would never come to an end, even as she prayed that they would. There was no winning.

Dylan had hurt her in a way only a person she was in love with could hurt her. That was another fact she didn't want to face, along with him thinking she had finally betrayed him, and her desperately not wanting to leave him.

She had argued with him two or three times, trying to make him see reason. He had been unwilling to join the fray, and she'd been left with nothing but a self-serving defense and her own paranoid delusions. If Dylan had been imagining the danger of the man in the restaurant, that was one thing. But if Charlie had gone bad, then they were walking into a setup they couldn't hope to escape alive.

"Dylan, you have to listen to me." She had sunk to pleading again, but this time her pride wasn't involved. "I'm not going with Charlie no matter what you say, so there is no reason for us to keep going. We can turn around and hide someplace else until we come up with another plan."

"No, we can't." He didn't sound very damn sure of himself, so she pushed.

"We have to. I'm not giving you a choice. I am not going with Charlie. I have reason to believe he's the one who leaked information, whether to Austin or the Bureau, I don't know, but—"

"Austin?" He turned on her. "You think Charlie Holter is working for Austin? Do you know what you're saying? I've trusted Charlie with my life, and he's never let me down."

"I'm looking at possibilities, that's all." For the first time that day she noticed a sheen of dampness on his forehead. She touched his arm, and even through his shirt she could feel him burning up. "You're sick."

She whispered the words in shock. As she looked him over more carefully a wave of guilt washed through her. She'd been so wrapped up in her hurt and anger, she hadn't noticed his sudden decline. He'd been fine when they'd stopped an hour ago for gas, she was sure of it. But he wasn't fine now.

The skin beneath his eyes was bluish and smudged looking. A thin line of sweat trickled down his hairline and darkened the already darker hair of his sideburn.

"We have to stop," she insisted, looking ahead at the city skyline as if a sanctuary would appear. The only beacon in the Seattle night was the Space Needle.

"If I stop now, we're both dead," he said. "The only chance you've got is to go with Charlie, and the only chance I've got is to not have to consider you. I need to get rid of you, Johanna, or I won't last the night."

Put like that, she had no choice.

"You can't just leave me in a bar somewhere without telling me when I'll see you again, or how I can get in touch with you." She knew she was sounding like a desperate woman about to be dumped—which was exactly what she was—but there was nothing she could do about it.

Dylan knew he could leave her without a word. He knew he *should* do just that. "I'll call you when things cool off." It wasn't much, but it was all he had to give her.

It wasn't enough.

"Liar." The word came at him softly from across the car.

He turned his head and saw her eyes close, saw the tear that slipped from beneath her lashes.

His hands tightened on the steering wheel. He swore to himself, and his hands tightened another degree. He'd thought he could go out with a good deed. He'd thought he could simply save her life and lessen all the regrets of the last years.

The more fool he.

FIFTEEN

Dylan went around the block twice, cruising from First Avenue to Pike Street and back again, looking for reasons to be jumpier than he already was. He found plenty, from the burned-out street lamp on the corner, which created an extra layer of shadow at the bar entrance, to the group of three casually dressed men loitering on the sidewalk, to the squad car pulled over to the curb.

The scene looked like the perfect setup, or a typical night in Seattle. He parked in the empty space behind the squad car when it opened up. The police weren't likely to shoot a woman, and they were likely to shoot anybody else who tried. It was the best he could do.

"When we get inside, I'm going to stay by the door," he told Johanna. "You go to the ladies' room. When you come out, if Charlie isn't right there, go sit at the bar and stay put. He'll find you." He lifted himself up off the seat and pulled a roll of bills out of his front pocket. "Here's three hundred dollars. Buy yourself a drink."

"Don't offend me. Please."

The coldness of her voice shook him at his core. What she was thinking wasn't so far off the mark. He did want to give her something in return for what she'd given him, but not money, and not for sex.

"Three hundred dollars wouldn't buy me a second look from you and we both know it, counselor," he said. "This is for taking care of me, because this is the only way I can take care of you after I walk out of that bar—and it's still damn little. If there's a problem, it will get you a cab ride and a room in the best hotel in Seattle. Do you want a gun?"

"Yes," Johanna said, fighting anger and tears, and trying not to shake so badly that he'd see.

"Do you know how to use it?"

"I shot a rifle once at a skeet range."

"It was a shotgun you were using, not a rifle," he chided gently, and she felt her last semblance of composure slip.

"Well, there you have it, then. I don't know a damn thing about guns, except I'm assuming it will have a trigger and that's the part I pull when I'm ready."

"You don't pull a trigger, you squeeze it. And if you wait until you're ready, you'll probably be dead."

"Excuse me," she said, her voice tight. "But if I'd known there was going to be a firearms examination at the end of the kidnapping, by God, I would have studied for it!"

Dylan pulled two handguns out of the duffel bag and loaded them, swearing softly and vehemently. Things weren't going well. Things weren't going well at all.

When he was finished loading, he handed one of the guns to her and stuck the other one in the waistband of his jeans, under his shirt. "Put it in one of the coat pockets. If you get nervous, either put the coat on and stick your hand in the pocket, or drape the coat over your arm and keep your hand in the pocket. Just make sure you have a hold on the gun and that it's pointing in the right direction before you squeeze the trigger."

She took the weapon without comment and did as he'd told her, slipping it into the coat pocket.

This was the moment to say good-bye, Dylan thought. There wouldn't be time once they got inside the bar. But he didn't know what to tell her and what to leave out. Everything had been going downhill so fast for him the last few weeks, even the last months, ever since Charlie had left. When Austin had put the hit on Johanna Lane, Dylan had felt the bottom fall out of his life. He had suggested a different way of dealing with her, but Austin had been adamant, and he had wondered aloud if his best man wasn't up to the job. There were others looking for a chance to move up.

Dylan had assured him he had no qualms. He'd told Austin he was the only one qualified not to screw up. He'd warned Austin against bringing in uninvolved outside help. In short, he'd all but begged Austin to let him have the opportunity to kill Johanna Lane. The memory still left an odd taste in his mouth. The scene had been surreal. After it was over, he'd had nothing left except the dead agents still hanging like a brace of albatrosses around his neck, and Johnny the Shark taunting him all the way to Lincoln, talking about his knife and the fun they could have with a piece like Ms. Lane.

It's a wonder the bastard had survived all the way to Nebraska.

Dylan glanced over at Johanna, but she wasn't looking at him. The angle of her chin told him she wouldn't either, but there wasn't a mark on her, and he took some pride in that.

He let out a heavy breath and looked back to the squad car parked in front of them. If he wanted to say good-bye, he was on his own, and he truly didn't have the strength for it. After he left the bar, he had to get well out of town, heading south, he'd decided. He would give Austin a call and wait for him in Portland. By this time tomorrow it would all be over, one way or the other—and that didn't leave him with a lot to offer her in the way of a good-bye or anything else.

"Okay. Let's go," he said, following the gut reaction that told him to skip the tears and just get the job finished.

They got out of the car and walked the half a block to the bar. Every step he took made him feel worse. She kept making these little sounds that were tearing at him. Soft sounds from her throat, as if she were struggling not to break down, and her arm was trembling within his grasp.

"You're going to have to do better than this, Miss Lane." He tightened his grip on her, trying to give her the strength he didn't have. "Charlie is fifty-two, five feet ten inches, one hundred and eighty-five pounds, most of it in a beer belly he's been building out of Red Hook Ale since he moved to Seattle. Short brown hair, kind of curly; blue eyes, round face. He looks like somebody's uncle. He doesn't wear glasses, but he always wears his monogrammed slicker. It says 'Holter Fishing Excursions, Charlie Holter, Captain.' That will be your big clue."

He got a tremulous laugh out of her, and he felt his mood brighten a notch above grim. They would get through this.

He pulled her close to his side when they reached the door and allowed himself to slip his arm around her waist. He hoped to catch her gaze and give her a meaningful look, whatever the hell that was, but she denied him again.

The bar was full to capacity, with standing room only and most of that taken. Cigarette smoke hung like a haze over the booths and tables. The bar itself was old teak and tarnished brass and the theme was definitely nautical. He checked the room, letting his gaze trail over the crowd, looking for trouble and finding none. He did see Charlie. The older man gave him the slightest of nods and shifted his own gaze to the bartender.

The deal was done.

"The bathrooms are at the end of the bar," he said. She nodded and started to pull away from him.

If she'd looked at him just once, he might have let her go. She didn't, though, and his control snapped.

"Dammit, Johanna." He pulled her back into his arms, forcing her to meet his gaze. *"I love you. You have to know that."*

Then he kissed her, once, short and sweet, taking his last taste.

Johanna couldn't see him through her tears when he let her go. She didn't want to see him. The whole situation was too awful. He was leaving her, leaving her so he could go die, and there wasn't a damn thing she could do about it.

A gust of fresh air blew against her face as the door closed behind him, telling her he was gone. She lowered her face into her hand and let the tears fall. *I love you too, Dylan Jones,* she thought. *I love you too.*

And she couldn't let the man she loved face Austin alone.

Her head came up. She wiped at the tears and looked across the jostling crowd to the bathrooms at the other end of the bar. She didn't know Charlie Holter, and she wasn't sure she trusted him, but he was the only chance Dylan had. If he was really Dylan's friend.

Keeping the coat close to her body, she shoved and sidestepped her way through the laughing, drinking people. When she reached the ladies' room, she stepped inside, took a breath, and came back out.

Come on, Charlie. Come on. We haven't got all night.
She moved back through the room, searching the faces around her, concentrating on the men at the bar. The instant she laid eyes on him, she knew she'd found who she was looking for.

His head came around as she approached him.

"Hello, Mr. Holter," she said.

He gave her a big smile. "Hi! It's good to see you." He lightly clapped her on the back in a gesture of friendship that Johanna didn't find reassuring.

"Our friend is in trouble," she said. "He needs help."

"That's why I'm here," Charlie said.

"Then let's go." She stepped out from under his hand and started for the door, but his hand came back down on her shoulder.

"I think we should wait," he said.

She turned and looked at him with all the authority she could muster. "If we wait, he'll be gone."

"That was the plan," Charlie countered smoothly.

"He needs help now, not tomorrow."

"Dylan can take care of himself."

"Not this time. He's hurt," she told him. "He's lost a lot of blood in the last couple of days. He's not very strong."

Charlie seemed to think for a minute, his blue eyes assessing her and what she'd said. "Okay," he said after a moment. "You win."

Johanna broke for the door, praying they weren't too late, but when she stepped outside, the first thing she saw was a station wagon backing into the parking space where the gray sedan had been.

Dylan was gone.

Dylan watched Johanna and Charlie exit the bar, and he watched the anguish come over her face when she realized he was gone. He wasn't sure why he'd waited, but looking at her made him think it hadn't been his best idea. He'd never wanted to cause her pain.

He had moved the sedan to the cross street closest to the bar where the shadows were deepest. The car was idling; he'd leave once he was sure she and Charlie had connected.

Well, he was sure, but still he didn't leave. He wanted to follow them, and only knowing he'd be increasing her danger, not lessening it, kept him from tailing her.

She and Charlie turned the corner onto the cross street where he was parked and started down the hill toward the market. Dylan would have left then— except for the man who came out of the bar next. Rodrigo, Austin's newest and brightest rising star, his dark hair slicked back off his face, his black suit double-breasted and formfitted.

Dylan's mouth went too dry for him to swear. At the same moment something coldly metallic pressed against the side of his neck.

"Austin is pretty disappointed in you, Dane," a man said from the backseat, "and we've got a score to settle for what you pulled coming out of that elevator in Boulder. I want you to head north on I-5."

"Hello, Jay," Dylan said, working to keep the fear out of his voice. Charlie had Johanna, and Charlie was working for Austin. It was unbelievable, but the truth was pushing into his neck. If it hadn't been for Johanna, he would have let Jay have him. Charlie Holter had gone bad. There was nothing left to trust in the world.

"Don't think you've got any help coming either," Jay said. "I got your friend."

Dylan didn't know who he was talking about. He could still see Johanna walking down the hill with Charlie at her side, being followed by Rodrigo. Austin was out there somewhere, too, but Austin was no friend.

"Where are we going, Jay?" he asked, shifting the car out of park with one hand while he reached for the gun under his shirt with the other.

"I thought we'd head toward Canada, get out of the city and into some country. Maybe we'll take a ferry ride—"

Five inches of upholstery buffered the sound of the shot. Jay slumped into the seat. Dylan threw the car back into park and disconnected the ignition wires in one fluid movement.

Ignoring Jay, he pulled the duffel bag up front and took out the shotgun, a box of shells, and an extra clip. He had to get to Johanna, and to do that, he had to take out Rodrigo and Charlie.

Charlie. The shock was numbing.

He got out of the car and walked down the middle of the street, almost a full block behind his quarry, angling himself closer to the line of parked cars. He had to move fast. Charlie and Johanna were already entering Pike Street Market, and all Dylan remembered about the place was how easy it would be to get lost in it. The market was closed this time of night except for a few restaurants, which only meant darker holes and more hiding places.

He would have preferred to keep everyone out in the open, but the only advantage he had was them thinking Jay had him driving out of town with a gun to his head.

Rodrigo had to be taken out first, silently.

Dylan kept to his side of the parked cars, staying low and moving quickly. His body told him it would never forget or forgive the punishment.

Charlie and Johanna disappeared into the market, and Dylan made his move on Rodrigo, coming up behind him and dropping him at the knees with a well-placed kick. Dylan let him fall to the ground, then came around to the side of him with the shotgun jammed in his ear.

"How many men does Austin have with him?" he growled, watching the man carefully as he picked up Rodrigo's gun.

"Five." The word was a bare gasp followed by a succinct curse. "I think you threw my knee out, Jones."

The use of his name brought Dylan up short. Rodrigo had only known him as Dane Erickson.

"Five including you and Charlie?" he asked.

"Five including Charlie and Jay, who Tom must have taken out or you wouldn't be here."

"I took out Jay," Dylan said, "and there wasn't anybody named Tom in my car."

Rodrigo cursed again, all the while lying on the sidewalk, grimacing. "So Jay got Tom, you got Jay, Charlie's got Johanna Lane, and you've got me, you stupid son of a bitch, but I'm on your side, so it doesn't count, unless you want to do me and explain it to Watkins later."

There was another name, Watkins. Dylan had tangled with his bureau chief more times than he cared to remember, and always to his detriment.

"You're FBI?" he asked Rodrigo.

The man nodded. "Charlie went bad. Nobody knew if you had gone over too. So they sent me in to watch you, and I'll be damned if I could tell. When you grabbed Johanna Lane, we thought for sure you were going to carry through on the hit. Then Austin found Johnny Shepherd, and we knew you needed help." Rodrigo looked up at him. "You're a damn hard man to help, Jones."

"Where is Austin waiting?"

"Bottom of the hill," Rodrigo ground out. "In a parking lot across from the wharf."

"Can you walk?"

In reply, Rodrigo pushed himself up, a laborious task that ate into Dylan's time.

"You don't have to worry about Austin," Rodrigo muttered, barely managing to stand. "We've got ten agents converging on him. The plan was for me to walk Charlie and Johanna in, with Tom as my backup after he'd made sure you were all right. The problem now is that Charlie still has the woman, and you and I are screwing around on this hill."

Dylan threw him his gun. "Back me up if you can," he said, then he went after Charlie.

Johanna's unease had grown to distrust with every step they took deeper into the labyrinth of Pike Street Market. When they'd first realized Dylan had already left, Charlie had immediately told her he knew where his ex-partner would go, especially if he was hurt. They had a good chance of catching up with him.

But Johanna didn't like the fact that Charlie Holter had parked so far away from the meeting place. He'd apologized profusely, explaining the difficulty of getting a good First Avenue parking spot anytime of the day or night. The lot below Pike Street didn't get nearly as much use, he'd told her, because people didn't want to climb the stairs that snaked up the long hill.

It made sense, perfect sense, and she didn't believe a word of it. Charlie had an answer for everything and he talked too much.

She stopped abruptly, all of her confidence centered in the gun she had in the palm of her hand, hidden inside the coat pocket—which was a damn poor place for her confidence.

"I'm going back up the hill, Mr. Holter. If you find

Dylan where you think you will, tell him I'm waiting for him in the place we discussed."

He looked at her for a moment, his smile unsure. "Dylan expects me to protect you, Ms. Lane. I can't do that if you walk out of here."

"I'm comfortable protecting myself." It was a lie. She wasn't comfortable. She was a nervous wreck.

"I can't let you go," he said, and her nervousness jumped the barrier into panic.

"I'm not giving you a choice." She pulled the gun out and backed away from him, making sure the gun was pointing in the right direction. Even if Charlie Holter turned out to be a saint, she knew she was making the right decision for herself. Her intuition was going haywire with all the emotional upheaval of the past two days, but she didn't like Charlie and she wasn't going anywhere with him. If she'd thought for even one minute longer, instead of jumping at the chance to find Dylan, she wouldn't have walked down the hill with him, let alone entered a deserted marketplace.

"Well, Ms. Lane, I'm not giving you a choice either." He pulled a gun on her, and she knew she wasn't in the presence of a saint.

They were in a standoff, until Dylan stepped into the picture.

"Drop it, Charlie."

"Dylan!" Charlie smiled, but he didn't lower his gun. "Tell the woman to relax, will you?"

"She's a lawyer, Charlie. She doesn't know how to relax."

Johanna didn't spare Dylan a glance. She was staring at Charlie's gun, wondering what would happen if she squeezed her trigger and missed him. Who would get hurt? Would she or Dylan die?

"This is no good, Dylan," Charlie said.

"I know about Austin," Dylan countered. "I know you left the Bureau to work for him. I should have figured you couldn't have bought your fishing boat on what the government was paying you, not the way you spend money."

"Get out of here, Dylan. Go." Charlie gestured with his free hand. "I only made a deal for the woman, not for you. We were together too long, partner."

"Dammit, Charlie. You know it doesn't work like that."

The distant sound of people running up the stairs gave them all pause.

"Get out of here, Dylan!" Charlie cried. "I saved your life too many times to watch you die tonight! Get out!"

Dylan didn't waver, and Johanna knew time had run out. Her hands trembling uncontrollably, she squeezed the trigger—and missed Charlie by a mile.

He swung on her, his gun leveled, and Dylan shot him. Two men broke from the stairway just as she was grabbed and dragged down from behind. She twisted her body to face her attacker and felt fear well up inside when she saw him. His black hair was slicked back off a decidedly Latino face, and all she could think was that he looked like somebody from a Colombian cartel, one of the Morrow Warner connections mentioned in the weekend newspapers.

With great difficulty he dragged her with him behind an empty wooden stall. She fought him all the way, until he managed to pin her beneath him and flash his identification.

"FBI, Ms. Lane. Stay down."

The marketplace sounded like a shooting gallery on the other side of the stall. Her heart was racing furiously. She didn't want to stay down. She had to know what was happening to Dylan.

The blast of the shotgun told her where he was. In the next instant he was almost on top of her as he slid into the place between the stalls.

"There's too many men out there," he said, talking to the FBI agent who was still holding her. "Your reinforcements have arrived, but I can't tell the good guys from the bad guys. I'm going after Austin."

"Dylan, no!" She lunged for him, but the man gripping her arm didn't give her a chance. Dylan slipped away from her, running for the stairs. He almost made it.

One second he was in control, and in the next he was knocked sideways by the bullet that hit him. She rose to her feet in slow-motion horror, watching as he fell, and fell, endlessly down the stairs, until he fell out of view.

"*Dyllllan!*" she screamed. "*Dyllllaaan!*"

SIXTEEN

"There never was a Dylan Jones, Ms. Lane, as I have already told you on numerous occasions. The man you knew was Dane Erickson, and he is dead." Chief Watkins was as polite as always, icily polite. "Your prying into this area will get you nowhere. If anything, I would think you'd be relieved to know the man who abducted you is gone."

Johanna knew he was gone. He'd been "gone" for two and a half months. But she didn't think he was dead. Austin Bridgeman was dead, though the account of his demise that the papers had given did not match up with the facts Johanna knew. Charlie Holter was dead, shot down by a man who'd trusted him implicitly and been betrayed, shot down to save her life.

But a man who had never existed couldn't die. That was the flaw in their reasoning, or a sign of her derangement. Most days she wasn't sure which.

She missed him with an ache that left her only in her dreams. She had gone on with her life, spending long weekends in Chicago with her parents, and the other four days in the newly redecorated offices of Wayland and Lane and in her apartment in Boulder. She wasn't sure why she kept coming back to Chicago, other than to harass Chief Watkins and to remember what it felt like to be safe. She didn't feel closer to Dylan there.

She had fallen in love out west, and after another weekend of trying to crawl back into the womb, she decided it was time to go home for good and stop leaning on her mother and father like a three-day crutch every week.

The plane ride back to Colorado was beginning to feel like a bus trip across town, she'd made it so many times since August. The holidays were coming, and she was going to try not to travel until they arrived. She'd never spent Thanksgiving or Christmas with Dylan, so the time of year shouldn't have been bringing extra sadness. It was, though. She could feel it creeping up on her with every passing day.

He'd told her not to forget him, and sometimes in the middle of the night she despaired that she never would be able to forget him. Their time together had been too intense, his leaving had been too sudden, too unresolved.

I love you, Johanna. You have to know that.

She knew it, and it was breaking her heart. She couldn't forget him. She couldn't let go of him. All she could do was find him.

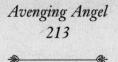

"This is crazy, Johanna," Henry said, dogging her steps into her office, crumpling the current page of their appointment calendar in his fist. "You can't have that man come here. Everybody will think we're involved in something sleazy."

"I am involved in something sleazy," she said, ignoring the pained expression her words brought to her partner's face. "A man who saved my life has either died or disappeared and nobody cares except me. It doesn't get much sleazier than that, Henry."

"You know what I mean." He threw the balled-up page into her wastebasket, then thought better of the action. "Having Albert Nathans come here is bad business. It doesn't look good." He bent over to retrieve the page, but apparently had no luck finding it. After tossing a few other papers out, he swore and went down on his knees to search through the basket.

"Mr. Nathans is an information broker, Henry. He is not a felon."

"Only because he hasn't been caught." Finding the recalcitrant page, he stood up and flattened it on her desk, smoothing it with his hand. "It's merely a matter of semantics."

"We're attorneys, Henry," she said dryly. "It's always a matter of semantics."

Using a pen off her desk, he began methodically blacking out the words detailing her two o'clock appointment. "I'm going to put this back on Mrs.

Hunt's desk, in the appointment book. I will be in my office when Mr. Nathans arrives, and I will remain there until after he leaves. My mother will be taking dictation for the hour."

"I think that's a good idea, Henry." She watched him scribble on the appointment page, then cast her eyes heavenward. Sometimes she didn't understand herself. How could she have possibly chosen Henry Wayland as her best friend and partner, then gone and fallen in love with a man like Dylan Jones?

Two weeks later the only question she was asking herself was how much longer she would keep trying before she accepted the truth. Mr. Nathans's highly unorthodox and probably illegal investigation had turned up five Dylan Joneses, none of whom had been her Dylan Jones.

He'd also found out that the FBI agent on the scene, Rodrigo Aragon, had been reassigned to some netherworld department in Washington D.C.

It was more than Watkins ever would have told her, but it wasn't what she'd wanted to know. She wanted to know where Dylan was—alive or dead. She had to know.

"The woman is damned persistent," Watkins said to the man across from him.

"How's the senator?"

"He'll come out in one piece, unless the Ethics Committee decides to actually do something." Watkins laughed, a deliberately wry sound. "Given that, if I was a betting man, I'd bet he'll come out in one piece and probably enjoy many years of continued service to the American people, except for the particular citizens he's giving us to hang on the Bridgeman cross."

"She's out of it, though, right?"

"You mean Johanna Lane?" Watkins asked.

"You know who I mean."

Watkins lowered his gaze for a moment before meeting the other man's eyes. "If everything you've given me pans out, she's home free. But it's going to cost you your job."

Now it was the man's turn to laugh as he pushed away from the table. "Don't do me any favors, like trying to get me reinstated. Okay?"

Watkins watched the man walk the length of the downtown Chicago restaurant, his stride taking him past highly polished dark wood tables laden with linen and crystal. Dressed in a suit and tie, he fit into the popular businessmen's lunch spot and watering hole like a hand into a glove. But Watkins knew it was all a facade. What he didn't know, what he would probably never know, was whether Dylan Jones had gone bad with his ex-partner and managed to cover his tracks, saving himself from Leavenworth by the skin of his teeth, or if he'd really been out there on his own for all those months.

Johanna hung the last ornament, a fragile crystal star, on her Christmas tree and stood back to survey her handiwork. She should have gone to Chicago. She shouldn't have stayed in Boulder with only Henry and his mother to fill in the empty places. She'd made some friends in the last few months and had a number of parties coming up, some social, some political, some business, most all three. She'd had her first Colorado date three weeks earlier, with a Boulder real-estate developer, an occupation, he'd explained, that made him a living contradiction. Everybody who moved to Boulder wanted to close the door behind them and shove home the dead bolt.

The date had been fine. The man had been charming, intelligent, and funny. He had not been Dylan Jones.

She was seeing a therapist again, trying to come to grips with a plaguing sense of loss, trying to find closure where there had been none. It was a long process at a hundred bucks an hour.

She took another step back, but it didn't help. Her tree looked exactly as it had the year before, and the year before that, and the year before that. She should have gone to Chicago.

The phone rang, and she reached behind her to answer it, keeping a critical eye on the tree. She was sure it looked exactly as it had the year before, which should have been impossible. Maybe she needed new ornaments.

"Hello?"

"Johanna."

The voice coming over the phone was unique, soft and gravelly, and it made her knees buckle. Her hand came up to her chest. She slowly lowered herself to the floor, before her legs gave way completely.

"It's Dylan," he said when she didn't say anything.

She nodded as if he were in the room.

"I'd like to see you."

"When?" she managed, forcing the word out around the million and one questions whirling through her mind.

"Tonight. Now. I'm only a block from your apartment. Did you have other plans?"

"No." She felt breathless. Dylan was alive.

"May I come over?" he asked after a short hesitation.

"Yes."

"Then I'll see you in a minute."

He hung up on his end, but Johanna forgot to do the same until the phone started beeping. Her hands shook as she placed the receiver back down where it belonged.

There were a hundred things she could do to get ready, and there was absolutely nothing she could do to prepare herself for seeing him again. In the end, nothing won out, and she was still sitting on the floor when her buzzer sounded.

She scrambled to her feet and raced for the intercom.

"Yes?" she asked, pressing the button down.

"It's Dylan."

She rang him up and stood by the open door, waiting for the elevator. When he stepped out, her knees weakened again.

It was Dylan.

She covered her mouth with her hand to keep back a sob. Then he had her in his arms, holding her, the two of them rocking together, with her crying and him talking to her softly.

"I'm sorry, so sorry." he said. "I wanted to call you so many times."

"Why didn't you?" she asked between the tears. "If you were alive, why didn't you come to me? You promised you would call."

"For a long time I didn't have a phone."

She lifted her head and looked into his eyes. He wasn't lying to her. There was nothing in his gaze except honesty and regrets.

"Why? Where were you? What happened that night?" Her questions tumbled over one another.

"Can we go inside first?" The barest smile touched the corners of his mouth.

They walked inside, still holding each other, and when the door was closed, she turned to him.

"If you want to kiss me, you better do it now, Dylan," she said, "because I'm going to be too damn mad at you later."

In answer his mouth came down on hers. He shrugged out of his overcoat and let it fall to the floor while he wrapped her in his arms.

It was a homecoming, the smell, and taste, and feel of her. She was everything he'd been without for too long. So he kissed her, and he kissed her again, and when she didn't resist, he slid his hands up under her shirt. He held her breasts in his palms, caressing the heavenly weight and softness of her, and he told her once more that he loved her.

She whispered his name and sparked a need inside him he didn't want to fight.

He hadn't intended to walk into her apartment and ravish her. He wanted to talk with her, and hold her, then make love with her if everything felt right. He wasn't sure what they had together, and he didn't think it was possible for her to know either.

But the heat of her response told him that like him, she needed more than a kiss to remake the closeness they'd shared. The warmth of her skin beneath his hands was the sign of life he'd sought in his mind all those months without her, and the way she trailed her lips over his face and neck was more than a physical gesture of desire.

"Shh," he whispered, kissing the tears off both her cheeks. "I'm not leaving until you ask me to leave. We have all the time you're willing to give."

"I missed you. I missed you so terribly, and now you're here, and I can't believe it, and it hurts. I'm so angry I could hit you."

She was babbling, her head buried into the front of his shirt, but she was entitled. They needed time. He held her and kissed her face and let her go on and on.

And on and on.

Eventually they moved to the couch, then Dylan managed to make a pot of coffee in her very fancy kitchen while she took a bathroom break. Later on they made sandwiches together. He told her about being shot in Pike Street Market and falling down the stairs, the concussion, the pain when he'd come around and found the agent in charge leaning over him, trying to decide if he'd live or not.

She told him Rodrigo Aragon had taken her out of the market the other way, back up the hill. They had cordoned off the stairs, refusing to allow anyone through. Henry had shown up the next morning and immediately asserted her rights.

"They took me to a Seattle hospital," Dylan said. "I was there for a week before they moved me to Chicago."

"How did your stitches heal?" she asked, curling her feet under her on the couch and taking another sip of coffee.

"Pretty good."

"Can I see?" She touched the front of his shirt, and his hand came up to cover hers.

"If you start taking my clothes off, counselor, I'm going to want to take you to bed," he told her, his voice growing husky.

A trace of color spread across her face, and she withdrew her hand. It wasn't the reaction he'd hoped for, but it was the one he'd half expected. She did have a shy streak, and that was okay. Life was stretching out before him brighter than it had in years. He could wait.

"What happened in Chicago?" she asked.

"Basically I was arrested. But they didn't have good evidence against me, and I had a whole lot of information they wanted. I told them I would give them everything they needed to get the senator talking to them, if they would give me you." He looked down at her and ran his hand over her shoulder. "I think I made a good deal. Of course, the Feds don't like their own people cutting deals with them, so I'm officially unemployed."

"I wondered why I hadn't heard from anybody about Morrow Warner," she said.

"You will, but only to a point. If it goes beyond verifying information, I can get it stopped."

She lowered her lashes and was quiet for a long time. "Where do we go from here, Dylan?"

"Nowhere, I hope."

Her startled gaze flew up to meet his, and he hastily explained.

"I mean that literally. I want to stay right here, on this couch, in this apartment, with you. But I know that's a lot to ask."

"You want to stay here with me?" she asked, surprise evident in the lift of her eyebrows.

"It's crossed my mind a few times," he admitted, then added slowly, "Especially tonight, though not necessarily on the couch."

Her color deepened, and he brushed his mouth over the tender skin between her cheek and ear.

"I'd like the chance to get worn-out making love to you," he said, kissing her even more softly. "I'd like the chance to get real bored watching you brush your teeth, and to reach my limit on sitting around reading with your feet in my lap. I'd like the most exciting thing in my life to be the moment I wake up and realize you're lying next to me . . . preferably naked, and warm from where I'd held you all night."

Johanna turned in his arms and settled her parted lips over his for a searingly intimate kiss. God, he was heaven to touch. She loved the differing textures of his skin, from the light raspiness of his cheek to the silken fullness of his tongue in her mouth.

He groaned, and she let herself lean more deeply into him. She wanted him in ways she'd never wanted another man, totally, possessively. When she lifted her mouth from his, she straddled his hips and began unbuttoning his shirt.

"Are you sure you want this?" she asked, looking at him through half-closed lashes.

"I'm sure," he said, so quickly she knew he'd misunderstood.

A smile teased her mouth. "I mean, are you sure you want to move in with me? I don't want to ruin us by going too fast."

"Johanna," he said, his eyes turning darkly serious. "I believe in love at first sight, and I believe that's what we've got going here. I was willing to die for you. I'm sure as hell not going to pass up a chance to live with you."

"Okay then, Dylan," she answered, finishing with his shirt and moving to the front of his pants. She undid the buttons at the top first, then slowly slid his zipper down, leaning forward to whisper in his ear. "Be sure and tell me when you get bored."

❖————————❖

Three months later Johanna dragged herself into the kitchen early on a Friday morning. She was wearing his baggiest, most stretched-out T-shirt, which looked like it had been slept in for a very good reason. She had on her own sweatpants and sweat socks. The ensemble was covered with a terry-cloth robe and topped with three sizes of hot curlers wound through her hair.

"Hey, houseboy," she said around a yawn. "Did you find a job yet?"

"Not yet, but I'm getting close." He held his cup up for a refill without lifting his eyes from the sports section of the newspaper.

She poured his coffee and got a cup down for herself. "What's for breakfast?"

"We've got my good cereal, which I would be willing to share. Or you can have your healthy cereal."

"I'll take the Frosty Crunchers." She sat down and inhaled the fuel-injected steam of Dylan's coffee while he poured her a bowl of cereal and milk.

"I like the porcupine look," he said. "It's very attractive, but you're losing a couple of quills on the left side."

She reached up and tightened the loose curler. "Are you bored yet?"

"I'm not sure," he said, snapping the paper back out. "I thought I'd watch you brush your teeth this morning. See how it works out before I make a commitment."

She grinned and waited for his eyes to appear over the headlines. She didn't have to wait long.

"What time do you have to be at work?" he asked.

Her smile broadened. "Don't you even think it. You know how Henry gets when I'm late."

"Yes," he said slowly. "But I also know how *you* get when I make you late."

"Save your strength for the weekend," she suggested, dipping her spoon into her cereal bowl.

"How would you like to be married to a lawyer?" he asked out of the blue.

She paused with her spoon halfway to her mouth. "I don't know," she said carefully. "I suppose it would depend on the lawyer."

He'd never mentioned marriage before, to anybody. She'd thought about it, though, a hundred times at least.

"Okay," he said. "How would you like to be married to a law student?"

"Are these hypothetical questions?" she asked. "Or are you coming to a whole lot of decisions all at once?"

"Neither. I've thought about going to law school for a couple of years. Then for a while there, I didn't think I'd live long enough to finish. As for the other, the first time I thought about marrying you was the first time we made love, and I've been thinking about it every time since."

"You've been thinking about it a lot," she said, impressed by just how much thought he'd given the subject.

"I guess the question then is, have you?"

"It's crossed my mind a couple of times," she

admitted, working hard to keep from jumping up and throwing herself into his arms.

"And what do you think?"

"I like law students," she said with a straight face. "I was one myself. As for marriage, well, I love you, Dylan, and nothing is ever going to change that."

"Then don't eat your Frosty Crunchers," he advised, and went back to reading the sports section.

Johanna looked down at her bowl. If she didn't eat them, they were going to get soggy. Even Frosty Crunchers would eventually succumb to milk.

But a diamond ring wouldn't . . .

Gasping, she reached into the bowl and pulled the ring out. She ran to the sink and washed it off before putting it on her finger.

"I can't believe you did that! Oh, Dylan, it's beautiful!" She spread her hand for him to see. "I can't believe you put it in my cereal bowl!"

"Pretty corny, huh?"

"And sweet and wonderful." She slid onto his lap and hugged him for all she was worth. "Oh, Dylan, yes," she said, then a moment later said, "Oh, no!"

"Which is it, Johanna?" he asked, setting her a little away from him so he could gauge the reaction on her face. "Oh, yes, or oh, no?"

"It's yes, a definite yes for marrying you, but I just realized you're making all my family's dreams come true."

"Your family has always dreamed of the day you'd find a ring in your cereal?" He sounded a shade skeptical.

"No, it's the law thing for my father. He's always wanted me to marry a lawyer. My sister has always wanted me to marry a lover, and my mother has always just wanted me to get married." She buried her face into her hands. "Lord, it's almost too bizarre that you, of all people, should turn out to be the answer to their prayers."

"I'm more concerned about being the answer to your prayers," he said.

She peeked at him from over the tops of her fingers. "You are, Dylan. Oh, you are. More so than I ever thought anyone could be."

"Good." His smile returned in full force, sexy and mischievous. "I think we can pretty much forget about getting boring from here on out." He began unwinding the curlers from her hair and dropping them on the floor.

"I'm going to be late."

He laughed softly and kissed her cheek at the same time as he gathered her T-shirt in his hands. "Don't worry. When the sign reads 'Wayland, Lane, and Jones,' I'm going to fire Mrs. Hunt and change the rules."

"You weren't kidding about not getting boring, were you?" she said, helping him by raising her arms over her head. The T-shirt came off, and she shook out her hair until it fell over her shoulders like a silken gold mantle.

"Life's an adventure, Johanna—God, you're beautiful," he said, pulling her into his embrace. "And loving you is going to be the adventure of my life."

THE EDITOR'S CORNER

The bounty of six LOVESWEPTs coming your way next month is sure to put you in the right mood for the holiday season. Emotional and exciting, sensuous and scintillating, these tales of love and romance guarantee hours of unbeatable reading pleasure. So indulge yourself—there's no better way to start the celebration!

Leading our lineup is Charlotte Hughes with **KISSED BY A ROGUE**, LOVESWEPT #654—and a rogue is exactly what Cord Buford is. With a smile that promises wicked pleasures, he's used to getting what he wants, so when the beautiful new physician in town insists she won't go out with him, he takes it as a very personal challenge. He'll do anything to feel Billie Foster's soft hands on him, even dare her to give him a physical. Billie's struggle to resist Cord's dangerous temptations is useless, but when their investigation into a mystery at his family's textile mill erupts into steamy kisses under moonlit skies, she has to wonder if she's the one woman who can tame his wild heart. Charlotte's talent shines brightly in this delicious romance.

New author Debra Dixon makes an outstanding debut in LOVESWEPT with **TALL, DARK, AND LONESOME**, #655. Trail boss Zach Weston is definitely all of those things, as Niki Devlin soon discovers when she joins his vacation cattle drive. The columnist starts out interested only in getting a story, but from the moment Zach pulls her out of the mud and into his arms, she wants to scorch his iron control and play with the fire in his gray eyes. However, she believes the scandal that haunts her past can destroy his dreams of happily-ever-after—until Zach dares her to stop running and be lassoed by his love. Talented Debra combines emotional intensity and humor to make **TALL, DARK, AND LONESOME** a winner. You're sure to look forward to more from this New Face of 1993!

Do you remember Jenny Love-Townsend, the heroine's daughter in Peggy Webb's **TOUCHED BY ANGELS**? She returns in **A PRINCE FOR JENNY**, LOVESWEPT #656, but now she's all grown up, a fragile artist who finally meets the man of her dreams. Daniel Sullivan is everything she's ever wished for and the one thing she's sure she can't have. Daniel agrees that the spellbinding emotion between them can't last. He doesn't consider himself to be as noble, strong, and powerful as Jenny sketched him, and though he wants to taste her magic, his desire for this special woman can put her in danger. Peggy will have you crying and cheering as these two people find the courage to believe in the power of love.

What an apt title **FEVER** is for Joan J. Domning's new LOVESWEPT #657, for the temperature does nothing but rise when Alec Golightly and Bunny Fletcher meet. He's a corporate executive who wears a Hawaiian shirt and a pirate's grin—not at all what she expects when she goes to Portland to help bail out his company. Her plan is to get the job done, then quickly return to the fast track, but she suddenly finds herself wildly tempted to run into his arms and stay there. A family is one thing she's never had time for in her race to be the best, but with Alec tantalizing her with his long, slow kisses, she's ready to seize the happiness that has always eluded her. Joan delivers a sexy romance that burns white-hot with desire.

Please welcome Jackie Reeser and her very first novel, **THE LADY CASTS HER LURES**, LOVESWEPT #658. Jackie's a veteran journalist, and she has given her heroine, Pat Langston, the same occupation—and a vexing assignment: to accompany champion Brian Culler on the final round of a fishing contest. He's always found reporters annoying, but one look at Pat and he quickly welcomes the delectable distraction, baiting her with charm that could reel any woman in. The spirited single mom isn't interested in a lady's man who'd never settle down, though. But Brian knows all about being patient and pursues her with seductive humor, willing to wait for the prize of her passion. This delightful romance, told with plenty of verve and sensuality, will show you why we're so excited to be publishing Jackie in LOVESWEPT.

Diane Pershing rounds out the lineup in a very big way with **HEARTQUAKE**, LOVESWEPT #659. A golden-haired geologist, David Franklin prowls the earth in search of the secrets that make it tremble, but he's never felt a tremor as strong as the one that shakes his very soul when he meets Bella Stein. A distant relative, she's surprised by his arrival on her doorstep—and shocked by the restless longing he awakens in her. His wildfire caresses make the beautiful widow respond to him with shameless abandon. Then she discovers the pain he's hidden from everyone, and only her tenderness can heal him and show him that he's worthy of her gift of enduring love. . . . Diane's evocative writing makes this romance stand out.

Happy reading,

With warmest wishes,

Nita Taublib

Nita Taublib
Associate Publisher

P.S. Don't miss the spectacular women's novels Bantam has coming in December: **ADAM'S FALL** by Sandra Brown, a classic romance soon to be available in hardcover; **NOTORIOUS** by Patricia Potter, in which the rivalry and passion between two saloon owners becomes the rage of San Francisco; **PRINCESS OF THIEVES** by Katherine O'Neal, featuring a delightfully wicked con woman and a rugged, ruthless bounty hunter; and **CAPTURE THE NIGHT** by Geralyn Dawson, the latest Once Upon a Time romance with "Beauty and the Beast" at its heart. We'll be giving you a sneak peak at these terrific books in next month's LOVESWEPTs. And immediately following this page, look for a preview of the exciting women's fiction from Bantam *available now!*

Don't miss these exciting books by your
favorite Bantam authors

On sale in October:
OUTLAW
by Susan Johnson

*MOONLIGHT,
MADNESS, &
MAGIC*
*by Suzanne Forster, Charlotte
Hughes, and Olivia Rupprecht*

*SATIN AND
STEELE*
by Fayrene Preston

And in hardcover from Doubleday
*SOMETHING BORROWED,
SOMETHING BLUE*
by Jillian Karr

Susan Johnson

Nationally bestselling author of
SINFUL and **SILVER FLAME**

Outlaw

*Susan Johnson's most passionate and richly textured
romance yet, OUTLAW is the sizzling story of a fierce
Scottish border lord who abducts his sworn enemy, a
beautiful English woman—only to find himself a captive
of her love.*

"Come sit by me then." Elizabeth gently patted
the rough bark beside her as if coaxing a small child
to an unpleasant task.

He should leave, Johnnie thought. He shouldn't
have ridden after her, he shouldn't be panting like
a dog in heat for any woman ... particularly for
this woman, the daughter of Harold Godfrey, his
lifelong enemy.

"Are you afraid of me?" She'd stopped running
now from her desire. It was an enormous leap of
faith, a rash and venturesome sensation for a woman who'd always viewed the world with caution.

"I'm not afraid of anything," Johnnie answered,
unhesitating confidence in his deep voice.

"I didn't think so," she replied. Dressed like a reiver in leather breeches, high boots, a shirt open at the throat, his hunting plaid the muted color of autumn foliage, he looked not only unafraid but menacing. The danger and attraction of scandalous sin, she thought—all dark arrogant masculinity. "My guardsmen will wait indefinitely," she said very, very quietly, thinking with an arrogance of her own, There. That should move him.

And when he took that first step, she smiled a tantalizing female smile, artless and instinctive.

"You please me," she said, gazing up at him as he slowly drew near.

"*You* drive me mad," Johnnie said, sitting down on the fallen tree, resting his arms on his knees and contemplating the dusty toes of his boots.

"And you don't like the feeling."

"I dislike it intensely," he retorted, chafing resentment plain in his voice.

He wouldn't look at her. "Would you rather I leave?"

His head swiveled toward her then, a cynical gleam in his blue eyes. "Of course not."

"Hmmm," Elizabeth murmured, pursing her lips, clasping her hands together and studying her yellow kidskin slippers. "This *is* awkward," she said after a moment, amusement in her voice. Sitting up straighter, she half turned to gaze at him. "I've never seduced a man before." A smile of unalloyed innocence curved her mouth. "Could you help me? If you don't mind, my lord," she demurely added.

A grin slowly creased his tanned cheek. "You play the ingenue well, Lady Graham," he said, sitting upright to better meet her frankly sensual gaze. His pale blue eyes had warmed, restoring a goodly measure of his charm. "I'd be a damned fool to mind," he said, his grin in sharp contrast to the curious affection in his eyes.

Exhaling theatrically, Elizabeth said, "Thank you, my lord," in a blatant parody of gratitude. "Without your assistance I despaired of properly arousing you."

He laughed, a warm-hearted sound of natural pleasure. "On that count you needn't have worried. I've been in rut since I left Edinburgh to see you."

"Could I be of some help?" she murmured, her voice husky, enticing.

He found himself attentively searching the ground for a suitable place to lie with her. "I warn you," he said very low, his mouth in a lazy grin, "I'm days past the need for seduction. All I can offer you is this country setting. Do you mind?"

She smiled up at him as she put her hand in his. "As long as you hold me, my lord, and as long as the grass stains don't show."

He paused for a moment with her small hand light on his palm. "You're very remarkable," he softly said.

"Too candid for you, my lord?" she playfully inquired.

His long fingers closed around her hand in an act of possession, pure and simple, as if he would keep this spirited, plain-speaking woman who startled him. "Your candor excites me," he said. "Be warned," he murmured, drawing her to her feet. "I've been wanting you for three days' past; I won't guarantee finesse." Releasing her hand, he held his up so she could see them tremble. "Look."

"I'm shaking *inside* so violently I may savage you first, my lord," Elizabeth softly breathed, swaying toward him, her fragrance sweet in his nostrils, her face lifted for a kiss. "I've been waiting four months since I left Goldiehouse."

A spiking surge of lust ripped through his senses, gut-deep, searing, her celibacy a singular, flamboyant ornament offered to him as if it were his duty, his obligation to bring her pleasure. In a flashing moment his hands closed on her shoulders. Pulling her sharply close, his palms slid down her back—then lower, swiftly cupping her bottom. His mouth dipped to hers and he forced her mouth open, plunging his tongue deep inside.

Like a woman too long denied, Elizabeth welcomed him, pulling his head down so she could reach his mouth more easily, straining upward on tiptoes so she could feel him hard against her, tearing at the buttons on his shirt so the heat of his skin touched hers.

"Hurry, Johnnie, please . . ." she whispered.

Moonlight, Madness, & Magic

by

Suzanne Foster, Charlotte Hughes, and Olivia Rupprecht

"A beguiling mix of passion and the occult. . . . an engaging read."
—*Publishers Weekly*
"Incredibly ingenious." —*Romantic Times*

This strikingly original anthology by three of Loveswept's bestselling authors is one of the most talked about books of the year! With more than 2.5 million copies of their titles in print, these beloved authors bring their talents to a boldly imaginative collection of romantic novellas that weaves a tale of witchcraft, passion, and unconditional love set in 1785, 1872, and 1992.

Here's a look at the heart-stopping prologue . . . .

OXFORD VILLAGE, MASSACHUSETTS — 1690 Rachael Deliverance Dobbs had been beautiful once. The flaming red hair that often strayed from her morning cap and curled in wispy tendrils about her face had turned more than one shopkeeper's head. Today, however, that red hair was tangled and filthy and fell against her back and shoulders like a tattered woolen shawl.

Prison had not served her well.

"The woman hath *witchcraft* in her," an onlooker spat out as Rachael was led to the front of the meeting house, where a constable, the governor's magistrate, and several of the town selectmen waited to decide her fate. Her ankles were shackled in irons, making her progress slow and painful.

Rachael staggered, struggling to catch her balance as the magistrate peered over his spectacles at her. Clearing his throat, the magistrate began to speak, giving each word a deep and thunderous import. "Rachael Deliverance Dobbs, thou hast been accused by this court of not fearing the Almighty God as do thy good and prudent neighbors, of preternatural acts against the citizenry of Oxford, and of the heinous crime of witchcraft, for which, by the law of the colony of Massachusetts, thou deservest to die. Has thou anything to say in thy defense?"

Rachael Dobbs could barely summon the strength to deny the charges. Her accusers had kept her jailed for months, often depriving her of sleep, food, and clean water to drink. In order to secure a confession, they'd whipped her with rawhide and tortured her with hideous instruments. Though she'd been grievously injured and several of her ribs broken, she'd given them nothing.

"Nay," she said faintly, "I know not of which ye speak, m'lord. For as God is my witness, I have been wrongly accused."

A rage quickened the air, and several of the spectators rose from their seats. "Blasphemy!" someone cried. "The witch would use *His* name in vain?"

"Order!" The magistrate brought his gavel down. "Let the accused answer the charges. Goody Dobbs, it is said thou makest the devil's brew of strange plants that grow in the forest."

"I know not this devil's brew you speak of," Rachael protested. "I use the herbs for healing, just as my mother before me."

"And thou extracts a fungus from rye grass to stop birthing pains?" he queried.

"I do not believe a woman should suffer so, m'lord."

"Even though the Good Book commands it?"

"The Good Book also commands us to use the sense God gave us," she reminded him tremulously.

"I'll not tolerate this sacrilege!" The village preacher slammed his fist down on the table, inciting the onlookers into a frenzy of shouting and name-calling.

As the magistrate called for order, Rachael turned to the crowd, searching for the darkly handsome face of her betrothed, Jonathan Nightingale. She'd not been allowed visitors in jail, but surely Jonathan would be here today to speak on her behalf. With his wealth and good name, he would quickly put an end to this hysteria. That hope had kept her alive, bringing her comfort even when she'd learned her children had been placed in the care of Jonathan's housekeeper, a young woman Rachael distrusted for her deceptive ways. But that mattered little now. When Jonathaan cleared her name of these crimes, she would be united with her babes once again. How she longed to see them!

"Speak thou for me, Jonathan Nightingale?" she cried, forgetting everything but her joy at seeing him. "Thou knowest me better than anyone. Thou knowest the secrets of my heart. Tell these people I am not what they accuse me. Tell them, so that my children may be returned to me." Her voice trembled with emotion, but as Jonathan glanced up and met her eyes, she knew a moment of doubt. She didn't see the welcoming warmth she expected. Was something amiss?

At the magistrate's instruction, the bailiff called Jonathan to come forward. "State thy name for the court," the bailiff said, once he'd been sworn in.

"Jonathan Peyton Nightingale."

"Thou knowest the accused, Goody Dobbs?" the magistrate asked.

Jonathan acknowledged Rachael with a slow nod of his head. "Mistress Dobbs and I were engaged to be married before she was incarcerated," Jonathan told the magistrate. "I've assumed the care of her children these last few months. She has no family of her own."

"Hast thou anything to say in her defense?"

"She was a decent mother, to be sure. Her children be well mannered."

"And have ye reason to believe the charges against her?"

When Jonathan hesitated, the magistrate pressed him. "Prithee, do not withhold information from the court, Mr. Nightingale," he cautioned, "lest thee find thyself in the same dire predicament as the accused. Conspiring to protect a witch is a lawful test of guilt."

Startled, Jonathan could only stare at the stern-faced tribunal before him. It had never occured to him that his association with Rachael could put him in a hangman's noose as well. He had been searching his soul since she'd been jailed, wondering how much he was morally bound to reveal at this trial. Now he saw little choice but to unburden himself.

"After she was taken, I found this among her things," he said, pulling an object from his coat pocket and unwrapping it. He avoided looking at Rachael, anticipating the stricken expression he would surely see in her eyes. "It's an image made of horsehair. A woman's image. There be a pin stuck through it."

The crowd gasped as Jonathan held up the effigy. A woman screamed, and even the magistrate drew back in horror.

Rachael sat in stunned disbelief. An icy fist closed around her heart. How could Jonathan have done such a thing? Did he not realize he'd signed her death warrant? Dear merciful God, if they found her guilty, she would never see her children again!

" 'Twas mere folly that I fashioned the image, m'lord," she told the magistrate. "I suspected my betrothed of dallying with his housekeeper. I fear my temper bested me."

"And was it folly when thou gavest Goodwife Brown's child the evil eye and caused her to languish with the fever?" the magistrate probed.

" 'Twas coincidence, m'lord," she said, imploring him to believe her. "The child was ill when I arrived at Goody Brown's house. I merely tried to help her." Rachael could see the magistrate's skepticism, and she whirled to Jonathan in desperation. "How canst thou doubt me, Jonathan?" she asked.

He hung his head. He was torn with regret, even shame. He loved Rachael, but God help him, he had no wish to die beside her. One had only to utter the word *witch* these days to end up on the gallows. Not that Rachael hadn't given all of them cause to suspect her. When he'd found the effigy, he'd told himself she must have been maddened by jealousy. But truly he didn't understand her anymore. She'd stopped going to Sunday services and more than once had induced him to lie abed with her on a Sabbath morn. "Methinks thou hast bewitched me as well, Rachael," he replied.

Another gasp from the crowd.

"Hanging is too good for her!" a woman shouted.

"Burn her!" another cried from the front row. "Before she bewitches us all."

Rachael bent her head in despair, all hope draining from her. Her own betrothed had forsaken her, and his condemnation meant certain death. There was no one who could save her now. And yet, in the depths of her desolation, a spark of rage kindled.

"So be it," she said, seized by a black hysteria. She was beyond caring now, beyond the crowd's censure or their grace. No one could take anything more from her than had already been taken. Jonathan's engagement gift to her, a golden locket, hung at her neck. She ripped it free and flung it at him.

"Thou shall have thy desire, Jonathan Nightingale," she cried. "And pay for it dearly. Since thou hast consigned me to the gallows and stolen my children from me, I shall put a blood curse on thee and thine."

The magistrate pounded his gavel against the table, ordering the spectators to silence. "Mistress Dobbs!" he warned, his voice harsh, "I fear thou hast just sealed thy fate."

But Rachael would not be deterred. Her heart was aflame with the fury of a woman betrayed. "Hear me good, Jonathan," she said, oblivious of the magistrate, of everyone but the man she'd once loved with all her being. "Thou hast damned my soul to hell, but I'll not burn there alone. I curse the Nightingale seed to a fate worse than the flames of Hades. Your progeny shall be as the living dead, denied the rest of the grave."

Her voice dropped to a terrifying hush as she began to intone the curse. "The third son of every third son shall walk the earth as a creature of the night, trapped in shadows, no two creatures alike. Stripped of humanity, he will howl in concert with demons, never to die, always to wander in agony, until a woman entraps his heart and soul as thee did mine—"

"My God, she is truly the devil's mistress!" the preacher gasped. A cry rose from the crowd, and several of them surged forward, trying to stop her. Guards rushed to block them.

"Listen to me, Jonathan!" Rachael cried over the din. "I've not finished with thee yet. If that woman should find a way to set the creature free, it will be at great and terrible cost. A sacrifice no mortal woman would ever be willing to make—"

She hesitated, her chin beginning to tremble as hot tears pooled in her eyes. Glistening, they slid down her cheeks, burning her tender flesh before they dropped to the wooden floor. But as they hit the planks, something astonishing happened. Even

Rachael in her grief was amazed. The teardrops hardened before everyone's eyes into precious gems. Flashing in the sunlight was a dazzling blue-white diamond, a blood-red ruby, and a brilliant green emerald.

The crowd was stunned to silence.

Rachael glanced up, aware of Jonathan's fear, of everyone's astonishment. Their gaping stares brought her a fleeting sense of triumph. Her curse had been heard.

"Rachael Dobbs, confess thy sins before this court and thy Creator!" the magistrate bellowed.

But it was too late for confessions. The doors to the courtroom burst open, and a pack of men streamed in with blazing pine torches. "Goody Brown's child is dead of the fits," they shouted. "The witch must burn!"

The guards couldn't hold back the vigilantes, and Rachael closed her eyes as the pack of men engulfed her. She said a silent good-bye to her children as she was gripped by bruising hands and lifted off the ground. She could feel herself being torn nearly apart as they dragged her from the meeting room, but she did not cry out. She felt no physical pain. She had just made a pact with the forces of darkness, and she could no longer feel anything except the white-hot inferno of the funeral pyre that would soon release her to her everlasting vigil.

She welcomed it, just as she welcomed the sweet justice that would one day be hers. She would not die in vain. Her curse had been heard.

"Fayrene Preston has an uncanny ability
to create intense atmosphere that
is truly superb."
—*Romantic Times*

Satin and Steele
by
Fayrene Preston

SATIN AND STEELE *is a classic favorite of fans of
Fayrene Preston. Originally published under the pseud-
onym Jaelyn Conlee, this novel was the talented Ms.
Preston's first ever published novel. We are thrilled to
offer you the opportunity to read this long-unavailable
book in its new Bantam edition.*

Skye Anderson knew the joy and wonder of love—as
well as the pain of its tragic loss. She'd carved a new
life for herself at Dallas' Hayes Corporation, finding
security in a cocoon of hard-working days and lonely
nights. Then her company is taken over by the leg-
endary corporate raider James Steele and once again
Skye must face the possibility of losing everything
she cares about. When Steele enlists her aid in
organizing the new company, she is determined to
prove herself worthy of the challenge. But as they
work together side by side, Skye can't deny that
she feels more than a professional interest in her

new boss—and that the feeling is mutual. Soon she would have to decide whether to let go of her desire for Steele once and for all—or risk everything for a second chance at love.

And don't miss these heart-stopping
romances from Bantam Books,
on sale in November:

ADAM'S FALL
a new hardcover edition of the Sandra
Brown classic!

NOTORIOUS
by Patricia Potter
The *Romantic Times* 1992
"Storyteller of the Year"

PRINCESS OF THIEVES
by Katherine O'Neal
"A brilliant new talent bound to make her
mark on the genre." —Iris Johansen

CAPTURE THE NIGHT
by Geralyn Dawson
"A fresh and delightful new author!
GOLD 5 stars"
—*Heartland Critiques*

and in hardcover from Doubleday

ON WINGS OF MAGIC
a classic romance by Kay Hooper

OFFICIAL RULES

To enter the sweepstakes below carefully follow all instructions found elsewhere in this offer.

The **Winners Classic** will award prizes with the following approximate maximum values: 1 Grand Prize: $26,500 (or $25,000 cash alternate); 1 First Prize: $3,000; 5 Second Prizes: $400 each; 35 Third Prizes: $100 each; 1,000 Fourth Prizes: $7.50 each. Total maximum retail value of Winners Classic Sweepstakes is $42,500. Some presentations of this sweepstakes may contain individual entry numbers corresponding to one or more of the aforementioned prize levels. To determine the Winners, individual entry numbers will first be compared with the winning numbers preselected by computer. For winning numbers not returned, prizes will be awarded in random drawings from among all eligible entries received. Prize choices may be offered at various levels. If a winner chooses an automobile prize, all license and registration fees, taxes, destination charges and, other expenses not offered herein are the responsibility of the winner. If a winner chooses a trip, travel must be complete within one year from the time the prize is awarded. Minors must be accompanied by an adult. Travel companion(s) must also sign release of liability. Trips are subject to space and departure availability. Certain black-out dates may apply.

The following applies to the sweepstakes named above:

No purchase necessary. You can also enter the sweepstakes by sending your name and address to: P.O. Box 508, Gibbstown, N.J. 08027. Mail each entry separately. Sweepstakes begins 6/1/93. Entries must be received by 12/30/94. Not responsible for lost, late, damaged, misdirected, illegible or postage due mail. Mechanically reproduced entries are not eligible. All entries become property of the sponsor and will not be returned.

Prize Selection/Validations: Selection of winners will be conducted no later than 5:00 PM on January 28, 1995, by an independent judging organization whose decisions are final. Random drawings will be held at 1211 Avenue of the Americas, New York, N.Y. 10036. Entrants need not be present to win. Odds of winning are determined by total number of entries received. Circulation of this sweepstakes is estimated not to exceed 200 million. All prizes are guaranteed to be awarded and delivered to winners. Winners will be notified by mail and may be required to complete an affidavit of eligibility and release of liability which must be returned within 14 days of date on notification or alternate winners will be selected in a random drawing. Any prize notification letter or any prize returned to a participating sponsor, Bantam Doubleday Dell Publishing Group, Inc., its participating divisions or subsidiaries, or the independent judging organization as undeliverable will be awarded to an alternate winner. Prizes are not transferable. No substitution for prizes except as offered or as may be necessary due to unavailability, in which case a prize of equal or greater value will be awarded. Prizes will be awarded approximately 90 days after the drawing. All taxes are the sole responsibility of the winners. Entry constitutes permission (except where prohibited by law) to use winners' names, hometowns, and likenesses for publicity purposes without further or other compensation. Prizes won by minors will be awarded in the name of parent or legal guardian.

Participation: Sweepstakes open to residents of the United States and Canada, except for the province of Quebec. Sweepstakes sponsored by Bantam Doubleday Dell Publishing Group, Inc., (BDD), 1540 Broadway, New York, NY 10036. Versions of this sweepstakes with different graphics and prize choices will be offered in conjunction with various solicitations or promotions by different subsidiaries and divisions of BDD. Where applicable, winners will have their choice of any prize offered at level won. Employees of BDD, its divisions, subsidiaries, advertising agencies, independent judging organization, and their immediate family members are not eligible.

Canadian residents, in order to win, must first correctly answer a time limited arithmetical skill testing question. Void in Puerto Rico, Quebec and wherever prohibited or restricted by law. Subject to all federal, state, local and provincial laws and regulations. For a list of major prize winners (available after 1/29/95): send a self-addressed, stamped envelope entirely separate from your entry to: Sweepstakes Winners, P.O. Box 517, Gibbstown, NJ 08027. Requests must be received by 12/30/94. DO NOT SEND ANY OTHER CORRESPONDENCE TO THIS P.O. BOX.

Don't miss these fabulous Bantam women's fiction titles

on sale in November

• NOTORIOUS

by Patricia Potter, author of *RENEGADE*

Long ago, Catalina Hilliard had vowed never to give away her heart, but she hadn't counted on the spark of desire that flared between her and her business rival, Marsh Canton. Now that desire is about to spin Cat's carefully orchestrated life out of control.

_____56225-8 $5.50/6.50 in Canada

• PRINCESS OF THIEVES

by Katherine O'Neal, author of *THE LAST HIGHWAYMAN*

Mace Blackwood was a daring rogue—the greatest con artist in the world. Saranda Sherwin was a master thief who used her wits and wiles to make tough men weak. And when Saranda's latest charade leads to tragedy and sends her fleeing for her life, Mace is compelled to follow, no matter what the cost.

_____56066-2 $5.50/$6.50 in Canada

• CAPTURE THE NIGHT

by Geralyn Dawson

In this "Once Upon a Time" Romance with "Beauty and the Beast" at its heart, Geralyn Dawson weaves the love story of a runaway beauty, the Texan who rescues her, and their precious stolen "Rose."

_____56176-6 $4.99/5.99 in Canada

Ask for these books at your local bookstore or use this page to order.

❑ Please send me the books I have checked above. I am enclosing $ _____ (add $2.50 to cover postage and handling). Send check or money order, no cash or C. O. D.'s please.

Name _____

Address _____

City/ State/ Zip _____

Send order to: Bantam Books, Dept. FN121, 2451 S. Wolf Rd., Des Plaines, IL 60018

Allow four to six weeks for delivery.

Prices and availability subject to change without notice.

FN121 11/93